CHAPTERS FROM AN AUTOBIOGRAPHY

The author at Glacier National Park, Montana, in 1935.

CHAPTERS
FROM AN
AUTOBIOGRAPHY

by

Samuel M. Steward

Grey Fox Press
San Francisco

Cover tattoo design by the author.

Library of Congress Cataloging in Publication Data

Steward, Samuel M
  Chapters from an autobiography.

  Includes index.
  I. Steward, Samuel M.—Biography.   2. Authors, American—20th
century—Biography.   I. Title.
PS3537.T479Z464   818'.5209 [B]   80-26602
ISBN 0-912516-59-3
ISBN 0-912516-60-7 (pbk.)

Distributed by The Subterranean Company,
P.O. Box 10233, Eugene, Oregon 97440.

FOR SCOTT

CONTENTS

NOTE

Someone once said that dead men tell no tales, but many of them have biographers who do.

I had always thought that you wrote your autobiography if a) your ego compelled you to think that if you hadn't been born, people would have wondered why; or b) your curiosity about the future had reached the vanishing point; or c) you had said everything else you wanted to say.

But several years ago a fourth possible reason appeared. Faced with an operation of some magnitude, I wrote everything down in case I should die on the operating table or be seized with total amnesia caused by some new-fangled anesthetic.

That autobiography was an horrendous thing: 110,000 words, three times as long as a porno novel; and in it I seemed to be trying to prove just how much I could remember—which was everything. It dragged; it was dull. The sweet gal to whom the agent had to submit it because of a contract obligation gulped several times and said that an audience for it might be difficult to find, since it fell (as it seemed) halfway between the literary and the homosexual. I forebore pointing out to her that only homosexuals and house-husbands could read nowadays, and consigned the thing to limbo.

Then a coupla things happened. Robert McQueen, the editor of the *Advocate*, began gently prodding me for an article, a memoir—and Richard Hall and I wrote one together on Thornton Wilder. And Robert went on gently prodding . . . Then Don Allen of the Grey Fox Press (a sly fox himself) waded through the original typescript, and gently said why not do thus and so with it? So I did thus and so with it, and most of the unnecessary words disappeared, although it is my sincere hope that in those remaining there is enough to offend every narrow-minded bigot twice over. And when it was all finished Don Allen said, twinkling, as he suggested the title: "Now the history is left open-ended, for the remaining twenty-three volumes."

So it is. But I really think there wouldn't be enough to fill more than fourteen.

So thanks to Robert and Richard, and Jim and Ike and Martin and Desmond and several Dons and their oh-so-gentle prodding.

S.M.S.

CHAPTERS FROM AN AUTOBIOGRAPHY

Chapter I

I ENTER THE WORLD

I N WINTER THE SNOW FELL thick in Woodsfield, melted for a day under a feeble sun, and froze again during the night. Then it was possible to take a toboggan holding about five persons, go to the top of Reservoir Hill at the north end of town, get on, and with a wild whooping go sliding down the street through town, a mile and a half, to the Catholic Church at the south end. Without knowing exactly why, I always managed to sit in front of the school's handsomest basketball player, who wrapped his long arms around me holding me tight, and pressed his long legs close against each side of my body. I was about ten years old.

Woodsfield, Ohio, was the county seat, a sleepy little town. It still is. It has grown worse; it has been arrested in time. Atop the county courthouse was a huge round dome in which were set four clock faces, and beneath the dome a columned structure housing a large bell. Since my father at one time was county auditor, I had access to this mysterious region; and after finding out what I was, and getting to the proper age, I used to take tricks up there.

I lived in a three-story house my Grandfather Morris built. Its small rooms were rented out to traveling salesmen (on whose laps I used to climb when I was very young); and there was a dining room where three meals a day were served. Thus my maiden aunts made a living for themselves and their parents—a rather cheerless existence of cooking and serving, making beds and washing, and tending the garden when there was time for it. There were many aunts in my life—some married and living elsewhere in the town, and three living in the Morris House. One—who died early, the one possessed of a great artistic talent—had once

1

been raped in a chickenyard by a wandering tramp. No one ever mentioned it, but everyone knew about it.

Luckily, not much of my childhood remains in my memory, but I think it was sheltered and pleasant enough. When I was three or four, I remember how painful it was when my mother held my hand as I walked beside her, for my arm was pulled straight up. In Richmond, Virginia, where we lived for a while because my father had one of his innumerable jobs there, I went across the street to a vacant lot and set fire to the dry grass. I also recall lying on my stomach reading a child's book about King Arthur while a few feet away my sister Virginia, five years younger, was on the potty, and a bit of poop exploded from her tiny behind, to fall directly on King Arthur's face. And once I was roller-skating on the street near a telephone pole, the kind that had climbing-spikes out the sides; a motorcyclist with goggles rounded the corner from Monument Avenue too fast, hit the curb and flew into the air. His skullpan was punctured on a spike. He hung there a moment and then fell to the ground dead, with brains and blood splattered all over the sidewalk. This accident furnished me with nightmares for a long time.

Once in Richmond we went to a carnival. There was a peaked building with the flags of all nations running to the top, at which point the Confederate battle flag waved in the breeze.

"But where is the American flag?" I asked my father.

"Shush," he said. "We are in Richmond."

There was a bully in our block. He used to pick me up by the ears. That hurt.

"Damnyankee," he said.

"Ow," I screamed. He would hold me for about twenty seconds.

My mother died in Richmond, of an intestinal obstruction. I was once permitted to go see her in the hospital. In those days children were still allowed to visit.

"Oh Sammy," she said. "I'm all cut up inside." This gave me a vivid picture of her belly cut into tiny pieces, and I wept. I was six. After her death, I was taken back to Woodsfield, where I lived until I was about seventeen.

One aunt, Ella, was more colorful than the rest. She married, but had no children, and lived to be almost ninety. She bought a new Buick every year, and drove it even after she began to have falling-down fits in the street. And one night this poor half-crazy old woman at eighty had to take a broom to fight a roomful of bats which had flown down from the attic above. One flew up under her skirt; she never quite recovered from the shock.

She and Uncle Will had a chickenyard behind their house. One day when I was seven, I went back there. Taken with an urge to pee, I pulled it out and let fly. The reigning rooster approached, and seeing what I suppose he took to be a little worm, gave it a mighty peck. I ran into the house hollering and bleeding, greatly shamed to be forced to tell them all how I had earned my place in the pecking order.

Thus I grew up amongst the women and it must have had some effect on me. My father didn't count, for he was a weak man and often absent traveling. Later when he was elected auditor I sometimes worked in his office, copying ledgers. Once I found a long list of names in a drawer.

"What are these for?" I asked, recognizing several of them.

At first he would not tell me, and then he did. "They're the ones that voted against me in the last election," he said, his face grown stormy, "and by God I'll get even with them all one day!"

As a child I had the usual diseases, plus some not so usual—a broken eardrum (treated with laudanum and pepper on a pledget of cotton), and rheumatic fever—which without antibiotics lasted a long time and was very painful, making it difficult to walk. I was much babied and coddled. I had mumps, chicken pox, measles four times, and a broken nose. The nose accident occurred when I ran into a board extending across a sidewalk, running with my head down. For two or three weeks I had two of the blackest eyes ever, and all my classmates in the third grade tried to find out who had socked me.

A fight? Not I, not ever. Once some bully picked on me when I was nine, and I ran screaming to my father.

"Teach me how to fight," I sobbed.

3

"Sorry, son—I can't," he said lamely. "You just have to make your hands into fists and keep them in front of your face. But the important thing is you must stand your ground."

Stand my ground, hell! Ever afterwards I ran from that particular oppressor, and never stood my ground for any physical fight. After a while I learned to talk my way out of difficulties.

Most of the townspeople thought me smart for my age. Perhaps I was. But I remember more disasters than triumphs. In second grade Miss Goddard asked me to stand and read a passage. It should not have given me trouble, but it concerned a horse and had the word "Whoa" in it which I pronounced "hoo—ay."

"Sit down, Samuel," she said, and called on Harriet Claugus.

Harriet had just come in from the country outside Woodsfield; she was considered a hick by all of us third-grade sophisticates. With her loping walk, her monkey-mouth with buck teeth, her braids and receding chin, she was the object of our cruel laughter.

A year after "hoo—ay," Miss Griffith in the fourth grade asked, "Who can give us an example of an exclamation in grammar?"

Harriet's hand went up. "Write it on the board, Harriet," said Miss Griffith.

Harriet wrote: "Pshaw, the building fell down."

Miss Griffith frowned. "That's not a strong enough word for such an event."

I put up my hand. "Yes, Samuel," Miss Griffith said. "What would you say?"

"God damn it, the building fell down," I said.

The effect was magical. Miss Griffith had a fit of coughing and hustled me out of the room to see the principal, who sent me home with a note, even though I tried to explain it was only something I had heard my father say. My Grandmother Morris, a very tiny woman but remarkably strong for her size, washed out my mouth with soap on a toothbrush. I can still taste it.

4

Woodsfield sprawled for a small town; the little white houses were far-spaced. Many streets were not asphalt, but honest red paving bricks. And it was a Wasp town—Methodists, Baptists, Presbyterians. The "Catlickers" were numerous, but never talked about their religion. Everyone was a little frightened of them—for were not the basements of church and rectory stacked with rifles and bullets against the day when they would take over the world? And were there not secret subterranean tunnels leading from the priest's house to the nuns' house, where vile things happened at night?

There was one Jew and his family. He was tolerated because he was a junk dealer—real junk, that is, the metal and rubber kind. And there was one black—a chiropractor. When I was nine, playing on Aunt Tillie's front lawn one afternoon, an old model T Ford sedan drove up and four men jumped out, dressed in white sheets and peaked hats. They ran into the black's house, seized him, and brought him out struggling. They drove off, leaving me paralyzed with shock. The next day his wife and child left, and Woodsfield's purity was once more established.

Cross burnings in empty fields were common; the Klan was strong. Years later, while I was working for an encyclopedia, an article on Ohio was sent in. The "authority" had written this: "The southeast corner of Ohio is possibly the most backward and culturally deprived section of the United States, worse even than Appalachia." We removed the sentence, but I knew what he was talking about. The physical isolation of the town (for the narrow-gauge railroad had disappeared, and then the bus) was indicative of its artistic, aesthetic, and intellectual isolation as well. But Monroe County had proudly named itself the "Switzerland of Ohio"—and the scenery *was* pretty—lots of wooded green hills and the Ohio River, blue-green in those days. And later on the farm boys proved handsome, and the town boys as well, as stalwart and ruddy as the real Swiss.

Perhaps the scenes of my childhood which I liked best were those of Jerusalem, Ohio—where we lived for a time, down the hill from Grandfather Steward's house. Our little shack-house had a "cellar"—built above ground and surrounded by a great mound of earth. Its floor was cool and damp to small bare feet, and the air breathed the faint earthy smell of potatoes, the odors of freshly churned butter, the richly fragrant apple-box, and the sharp smell of the vinegar barrel, with the can standing under the spigot.

I loved going up the hill to Grandma's house through the rows of corn, the swords of the leaves rustling like a roaring of distant water. The trip was an adventure, as I looked for field mice, listened to the bobwhites, and watched the browning tassels sway in the wind. In the kitchen there was the odor of the oilcloth on the table, the smell of butter and fresh-baked bread; and in the closet where Grandfather—a horse-riding country doctor—kept his boots, saddle, and whip there were the sharp and sexual smells of leather and horses. In the darkened parlor there was a pedal organ with yellowing keys, stereopticon picture cards, a centipede sealed in a heavy glass hemisphere, dried plants in vases, and the horsehair sofa with the scorched top-edge where some ball lightning had once come in the window and rolled along its length . . . after which Grandfather put lightning rods on every gable of the house.

Outside under a fragrant grape-arbor, with the leaves making a green roof and a green shade, a foot-propelled swing stood with the trumpets of morning glories alongside a picket fence. And there, too, on a memorable Sunday afternoon when all the family except me had gone to a "temprunz" meeting in the Methodist church, stood a barrel of cider turning to the winter's supply of vinegar. I had been left behind, for at five years I was too young to understand what it was all about.

It was a balmy day. The wind blew lightly over the cornfield and was cool under the flat-topped arbor, which was heavy with fragrant silvery-purple clusters of Concord grapes. The barrel represented cider to me. I ran to the barn for some straws, brought a footstool from the kitchen, climbed up on the barrel and hammered out the bung. Then I straddled the barrel, inserted the straws, and drew deep. It was good, very good—but a little strange: it stung my mouth a bit.

When the family got back from the meetin', there was little Sammy lying on his back beside the barrel and gazing up at the grape leaves, burbling happily and gurgling at the patches of blue sky.

A horrified shriek burst from someone as I was yanked to my feet.

"Land o' Goshen!" said my Grandmother Steward. "The boy's *drunk!*"

That was the first time I took the Daughter of the Vine to bed. But I had had an example to follow: my father, the boozin' side of the family. Everyone else was arrayed on the other side—teetotalers all.

By the time I reached the eighth grade in school, at the advanced age of fourteen, one might think that some of the delights of sex would have unfolded for me.

Not so. One afternoon the principal, a dour-faced man, gathered all the eighth-grade boys in a room. The knowledgeable ones knew what was coming. I didn't.

Cyril Dougherty poked me in the ribs. "This is the day we learn all about life," he said.

"Uh, ha-ha, yes," I said.

The only thing remembered from that talk was that the principal spoke of the danger of "touching oneself *down there,*" which he said while one hand vaguely swung in the segment of an arc in front of his own crotch. The room was hushed.

As we marched down the sidewalk after school, Cyril said: "Imagine—Clark Loper didn't know what ole W. J. was talkin' about."

"Ha ha," I said. Neither did I. But in my sheltered little-boy Methodist way, the talk caused me much agony. The slightest brushing of my hand against my penis was not only a religious sin, but would lead to blindness and pimples, kidney disease, bed-wetting, stooped shoulders, insomnia, weight loss, fatigue, stomach trouble, impotence, genital cancer, and ulcers.

And then a wicked redhead, Bill Shafer, showed me what W. J. was really talking about. He introduced me to fantasyland and showed me a new device for my solitary hours

7

with his none-too-specific instructions: "You just keep going back-and-forth on it, like this, and you'll see what will happen."

Wicked Bill, delightful Bill—thanks a lot forever and ever! Alone in the Morris House bathroom I kept going back-and-forth on it, and suddenly my whole body began to tingle, and the tingling raced from head to feet. My breathing stopped, and like a strongly-pulled bow my body bent almost double over the toilet to release the four magic drops. Then with senses reeling, heart racing, panting, I fell back against the door until the black-red specks stopped dancing before my eyes.

Marvel of marvels! Was it sinful? Who cared? It was a skill that would always be with me. My rod and my staff would comfort me. I set about learning more, but that was difficult in rural Ohio in those years. The movie house owner showed an animated film one day (males on Tuesday, females Wednesday) about reproduction. But the females never got to see it; the uproar over the first showing nearly got the old guy lynched.

Most of the boys carried a rubber, which they had bought from the town's "agent," a young barber named Charlie.

I bought some, three for a dollar—expensive in those days. They came rolled in a small round tin box embossed with "Three Merry Widows. Agnes. Mabel. Beckie." (A thousand years later I found one of those boxes at a flea market, and bought it from an unsuspecting straggle-beard for a quarter.) I was not yet brave enough to try anything with Agnes, Mabel, or Beckie, except to wear one of them while practicing the shafer ritual.

Among my classmates there were two girls who had scarlet reputations. One was Gwendolyn, a flamin' red-hot mama. She played jazz piano wonderfully well, much better than I ever could, although I rippled a mean "Rustle of Spring." But Gwendolyn snubbed me. She preferred Ralph Truex, a dark Heathcliff sort of man with curly black hair and a sexual aura. I preferred him too, but didn't know why. My fantasies during shafer-time placed Ralph on top of Gwendolyn—but she was a blur, whereas I could see every

8

hair on his ass and every muscle in his legs and back.

My Aunt Minnie sighed. "Why can't you take up with a decent girl like Kathryn?"

Kathryn was an intellectual rival. We were the two smartest students in first year high school. Everyone thought we would get married and produce brainy children.

"She's got pimples on her chin," I said.

"Never mind. They'll go away."

But Kathryn got knocked up by Lou, a boy with whom I had been shafering.

Then there was Edith, another fast one according to rumor. In Edith's front parlor one night we got pretty far. In order to keep myself from getting a disease and also from messing up my trousers, I put on both Agnes and Mabel at the same time, figuring that afterwards I could remove Mabel and wear Agnes until I got home to wash.

Unfortunately, the mechanics of getting both on made Edith titter and ask what in the world I was doing. Hearing that, I was immediately deflated. Nothing thereafter could be done. Burning with anger and shame I fled the scene— and then, as if by magic, my manhood asserted itself in the privacy of my bedroom and Agnes got what was coming to her.

Finally, I developed a crush on a lady teacher named Buddy Starner—small and blonde, with peachbloom skin and blue eyes, the typing teacher. She accepted my homage gracefully, and since her morals were impeccable, I was allowed to spend hours with her in her apartment, playing "The Rosary" by Ethelbert Nevin. She was my ideal, although I had no idea what to do with her. Had not Fate stepped in, I might still be in her parlor playing.

One afternoon when I was not expected, I stopped at her rooms. The door was partly open. Standing on tiptoe was my beloved Buddy Starner in the arms of the dark Heathcliff man, Ralph Truex. I was destroyed, but my circular rationale made me conclude that if both Buddy and I liked Ralph, and if Ralph and I had both fallen for her, then probably Ralph and I had similar tastes; if he likes Buddy, then he might like me too.

I confronted her later and asked if she were going to marry him.

"Heavens no!" she said with a cascade of silver bells. "He's only eighteen." Then she changed the subject. "Coach Johnson asked me the other day why you didn't try out for the track team."

"I can't run all that fast."

"He said he saw you running up the alley the other night, and you went like the wind."

A compliment from the Coach pleased me, even if he had seen me leaving Edith's place, for he looked a lot like Ralph Truex—the same black curly hair, and—seen once in the gym showers—a sturdy well-muscled body with a fan of black hair on his chest. I went to see him and he talked me into trying out. I did, my specialty becoming the hundred-yard dash. The Coach was delighted with me, and I hungered for his approval.

But when spring came, it was time for the various teams to have their pictures taken. I refused to get into my track costume and join them. The Coach was upset.

"Come see me this afternoon after football practice and we'll talk about it."

Nervous, I went to his office in the basement of the school. There was a sign on his door saying: "Am in the showers. C.L.J."

The note did not say "Come see me" nor "Wait for me."

With dry mouth and pounding heart, not knowing what he meant me to do, I finally went towards the showers with hesitant feet, urged on by some deep power.

Standing outside the steamy door I heard water running, and a tuneless humming. I pushed the door and went in, around the corner to the three shower stalls.

"Hullo there!" the Coach called in a loud cheery voice. My knees were weak.

"H-Hul--lo," I managed to answer.

We were alone in the room. His muscular tanned body turned actively under the shower as he soaped himself, his arms and chest. His black curly hair was flattened by the water running down the sides of his handsome darkbrowed face. My eyes took in the length of his superb body, the sturdy thighs, the well-developed calves. I could hardly bring myself to look at his genitals, swinging free. But in his soaping, he turned his attention to them, pulling, washing . . .

The room began to turn opalescent in the corners, my breathing grew short, and then with a rush the black spots came from all the inside edges of the room-cube and blotted out my sight . . .

I had fainted. It did not help much to be revived and see the Coach straddling me naked, water from his body dripping on me, a worried frown on his face.

"What happened?" he said.

"I-I g-guess I f-fainted," I said weakly.

"Does this happen often?"

"N-no," I managed. "I'll be all right." I got to my feet and summoned enough courage to look at his naked body, but did not dare let my eyes go below his heavily muscled gleaming shoulders. "I f-forgot to eat lunch," I said.

"Well, get something in your stomach right away," he said gravely.

I wonder if he knew, if he were playing games with me. I'll never be sure. I guess it wouldn't matter anyway; he would be eighty now.

It was gradually becoming clearer to me what I wanted. And it was equally clear to me, then and now, that I had absolutely no choice in the matter. The grace of the male has always far outshone that of the female for me. I was different—a queer alone in a world of gash-hounds—or so I thought at the time.

Little things helped me along my alternate path. An older boy went to Buckeye Lake, a summer resort, and returned with tales of how a fairy had given him a tongue-bath and sucked his dick. I tried this immediately in the attic of the Morris House with a highschool fullback, who had a high rose color in his cheeks and wore his hair in a pompadour. And there on a sheeted mattress amidst the dust and cobwebs, the morning stars sang together for the first time for me—for a period of about two minutes, since the football hero was very quick on the trigger.

Now I knew what I wanted, but hardly how or why. And then a second event occurred, so unusual and bizarre and coincidental that it would not be believed in a work of fiction. Passing a room in the Morris House vacated by a salesman, I saw a book under the bed. It had evidently been stolen from the state library in Columbus—so the card in the front flap indicated. Stamped on the inside front cover was a word in large blue capitals: "Restricted." The book was one of Havelock Ellis' *Studies in the Psychology of Sex*, Volume II, Sexual Inversion.

The book opened the wide tall doors of the world for me, for it seemed that Ellis had gathered all sex together in one place. Not only did I discover that I was not insane or alone in a world of heteros—but I learned many new things to do. I made a secret hiding place for the book under the attic stairs, and read and read and read.

Thus I became an expert in the field of theory (by the time I finished the book I probably knew more about sex than anyone else in the county) and then began to make practical applications of this vast storehouse of material. For the most part I easily found willing bodies to practice on—four members of the football team, all of the basketball, three of the track—and curiously, no one taunted me, nor was I openly called fairy or sissy or pansy or queer. I think that the healthy young Ohio animals enjoyed it. There was Ted, who spread his heavy young thighs on carefully arranged red velvet curtains in the house of an elderly couple gone to Florida for the winter; and Kenny—a cropheaded crewcut blond in a Ford at the foot of Gooseneck Hill—an appreciative sort, the first one to kiss me after the labors were done. And the cousins Earl and Carl—Carl with the dusky brown-rose complexion, the first to reciprocate. And Fred, Ted's brother—smooth and sophisticated, the town sheik with his slicked-back hair and handsome well-made body—spending his weekends in Wheeling, West Virginia, going from one whorehouse to another . . .

I chanced to meet Fred on a wet and drizzly evening in front of the postoffice. Chanced? I had been stalking him since early afternoon. Light poured from the window full on his face. He wore a yellow rain slicker, and no hat—very daring for those years.

And how to get this hero for myself?

A direct approach—no euphemisms. Right straight out with the four-letter words, the language of love in the 1920s. I told him what I wanted to do.

He cocked one eyebrow. I saw the little hairs of it glisten in the light with tiny water-beads of drizzle. He smiled crookedly. "I heard you were up to that," he said. "What's in it for me?"

My first hustler . . . "Well," I said, swallowing with difficulty. "I could probably get you a quart of red wine" . . . steal it from someone's cellar.

"Okay," he said. And so it was up to the courthouse tower, a few feet above the stained glass skylight and a few feet under the great bell, with Fred astride a beam. Fred came just as the clock struck eight, and the double surprise nearly knocked both of us off the perch.

Another favorite trysting place was the new cemetery— the old one being too close to the streetlights. I favored a tombstone of the proper height so that I could stand and my conquest could sit. Was there some kind of obscure challenge at work, to make me select such a place? An affirmation of aliveness, of sex and joy, in the midst of death? Years later, the chill came on me when I read the last sentence of Thomas Mann's *The Magic Mountain*:

Out of this universal feast of Death . . . may it be that one day Love shall mount?

Certain friends were taken to certain places, and the Sunday-school classrooms in the balcony of the Methodist Church were one. Lou, who married Kathryn, was a haymow partner, and my memories of him were associated with hayseeds and straw in my hair and spiky feelings in my palms and kneecaps.

Out of this universal feast of love, however, arose a mistake which I should have foreseen. Made careless by a succession of triumphs, I wrote a note to a salesman in the Morris House and left it in his room. I can see him now! as I

13

looked down from between the rungs of the upstairs banister-railing, the white skin and copper-colored hair, the smooth and polished muscles as he returned from the washroom, clad in trousers and sleeveless undershirt, to the privacy behind his solid wooden door.

The salesman left the next morning, two days before he had planned. He took the note to a restaurant, and the owner took it to my father. The worst had happened.

For some years I had tried to love my father, but it never worked. We fought continually. Once, a long time before, both he and I had taken the same IQ test, and my score when adjusted for age surpassed his. He never seemed to forgive me . . . jealousy, perhaps.

When he came home from work that evening he was glowering. "What are you doing tomorrow?"

It was Saturday; I was working in Uncle Will's grocery store. I told him. He took three dollars from his pocket "Tell your uncle you're sick," he said. "We're going to take a ride tomorrow."

"I get only two," I said, and handed one bill back. He took it.

We started early. He was silent, and I was terror-struck. It was a miserable two-hour drive through the lovely green countryside. He went to the right when we reached the river, drove a mile and stopped. He turned to me. I must have been white-faced. I looked straight ahead.

"Now then," he said. "What's all this about your wanting to do something vile with that Rensaleer fellow?"

"Who told you?" I countered.

"None of your gah-damned business," he said. "I want to know what the hell a son of mine means by writing love letters to another man."

"I think," I said, drawing on my new vocabulary from Havelock Ellis, "that I am homosexual."

"Homosexual? What the hell's that?"

"It refers to the love that dare not speak its name," I said, remembering Wilde. "It is the same emotion that Socrates felt, and Michelangelo. It—"

"Don't give me any of your smartaleck highschool

14

rhetoric!" he bellowed. "Are you a cocksucker or not?"

"I've never done anything like that," I said, batting my eyelashes. "I just feel . . . well, I feel *drawn* to men."

"What men?"

"Well, Coach Johnson," I said, "and maybe Ralph Truex . . ."

"Did you ever . . . *touch* those men?"

"Why, I suppose I have," I said innocently. "I've shaken hands . . ."

"Goddamnit, you know what I mean!" he roared.

"No, not that way," I said, making myself tremble a little.

So it went for a half hour. When I saw that he wanted to believe that I had not actually sinned, the game became fairly easy, for I was already schooled in duplicity. I pretended to be chastened, to be horror-struck at the enormity of it (he told me of the Ohio law—twenty years penalty), and to show a firm purpose of amendment, as a good Catholic might say. I was protected in another way—midwest American views on homosexuality in the 1920s were very quaint, and were based on the assumption that all people raised in civilized Christian countries knew better than to fall in love with, or bed, persons of the same sex. Knowing better, then, the fundamentalist mind made two breathtaking leaps of illogic: people did not do such things, and therefore such things must be nonexistent. This kind of thinking protected us all during the 1920s and 30s. Though one might be teased for being a sissy, no one could believe that any person actually engaged in the "abominable sin." We lived under the shadow and cover of such naiveté. Only when the audience grew more sophisticated did the long ordeal begin once more.

Having found the role my father wanted me to play, I worked it to the hilt, falling in easily with his suggestion that perhaps I should go to see a professional whore—that such an experience might start me on a heterosexual (he said "normal") path. That evening I met one of my favorites, Carl, and had a romantic encounter with him under the stars. Afterwards, I told him about the day's experience. I knew he would keep quiet; he was as deeply involved as I.

15

"Tell you what," he laughed. "Next weekend we'll drive to Wheeling and visit a real whore."

"I don't particularly want to," I said.

"Oh, come on—try it once," he said. "It'll be fun."

"I'll probably be thinking of you while I'm with her," I said, with a sudden flash of insight.

Carl laughed. He had the biggest collection of beautiful white teeth I had ever seen, shining against his dusky skin.

"That's all right, too," he said. "Maybe I'll be thinking of you. Your mouth."

I left a note for my father asking for the loan of five dollars, to do "what we were talking about last week." We had to communicate by notes since he was working nights.

The next morning I found his reply: "If you think for one minute I'm going to give you any money to go to Wheeling to get the clap or syff, you're badly mistaken." No "Dear Son," no signature, no money. I borrowed five from an aunt and we went anyway. But we pulled off on a road the other side of Barnesville, because Carl had got so warmed up thinking about the coming encounter that he had to be cooled off.

The visit to the whore was a sad little experience. Carl went into one room with a girl, myself into another. It took me a long time—and finally the girl herself had an orgasm. My own was brought about by thinking of Carl, as I had foreseen. Afterwards, the girl squatted above a round white enamelware basin on the floor filled with a pale blue solution, copper sulfate I presumed, and with both hands splashed the liquid vigorously into herself.

Outside, Carl was talking to his girl. "What took you so long?" he asked. "I was done in five minutes."

"I wanted her to get her money's worth," I said archly. They laughed.

My father never mentioned the episode again. As for myself, after the shock wave passed, I went on just as blithely as before. In the summer of 1927 my two aunts, in their sixties, sold the Morris House and bought a modest home in Columbus, Ohio, to put my sister Virginia and myself through highschool and the university by taking in students as roomers. I severed all emotional contacts with Woodsfield.

16

True, I went back now and then to bury a relative, but all neural connections between the town and myself had been forever destroyed. I was a stranger in a strange land when I returned. Whether word of my obliquity had been passed around I neither knew nor cared.

So farewell, Woodsfield, farewell! I could perhaps stay within your limits forever, going on and on, filling volume after volume like old Proust sitting with shrunken shanks in his tub of tepid bathwater, gargling it and spitting it out and gargling again—all that dreadful curdled residue of the past.

But there must be an end to childhood—and to gargling. The birth of desire had taken place in me, and the patterns that I needed to survive were firmly imprinted by the time I left the town: concealment and pretense, duplicity, a guise of wide-eyed innocence—and a kind of "passive aggression" that was not expected in such a shy-seeming young man. I went to Columbus with the major purpose of bringing pleasure to others, mainly straight young men, and not to be concerned about pleasuring myself—for in bringing it to those I admired, I *did* please myself. In all the encounters since then, until—as Sophocles said—age released me from the tyranny of the mad master, sexual desire—I did the asking, and more often than not, succeeded.

Another aim? Oh, yes—nearly forgotten: to get an education.

Chapter II

UNIVERSITY YEARS

H OW ROMANTIC THE CAMPUS OF Ohio State University seemed to me, and the abundant life that it contained! The buildings crouched around the green and grassy Oval, beginning with the medieval armory—a turreted and castellated red-brick building looking as if it had been directly transplanted from Camelot. The library was at the far end; midway on the left side was the old ivy-covered geology building, housing the campanile which was played every day at noon. Remembering all of it transports me back a couple of centuries and a thousand beddings, to another continuum in time—to a few hazy dim and golden wonderyears, a green campus, frats and dances and young lovers sitting on the benches around Mirror Lake in the blue and windy twilight—a life of genuine excitement when the dawns were lemon-chill, sparkling and immortal, and the sunsets riper than garnets and Orient-lush with the sexual promises that every evening held.

I did not burst upon the academic scene with the flash and exuberance of a splendid rocket emitting golden stars in a brief path across the heavens. But although it was unknown to me at the time, my arrival did occasion something of a stir amidst certain arcane circles.

Part of the entrance requirements was the writing of an essay on your choice of subject, so that you might be placed in the proper class level of freshman English. I chose Walt Whitman as a topic, and let fly with all the accumulated but undigested wisdom—and none of the caution—of an eighteen-year-old who had read Havelock Ellis, and also through him investigated John Addington Symonds and found out about Horace Traubel and Peter Doyle. Moreover, instead of writing on *Leaves of Grass* in general, I chose the homosexual "Calamus" section in particular. I analyzed

Whitman's praise of the "manly love of comrades," connecting it with his duties as a Civil War nurse, quoted *The Invert* (by "Anomaly") on why inverts made such good nurses, and damned the highschools for teaching nothing of Whitman's but "O Captain, My Captain" and the lilac poem.

This amazing little essay I later learned landed in 1927 in the midst of a staidly closeted English department with the disruptive force of several pounds of TNT. It was discussed for days, and none of the overly cautious teachers would touch me with a long pole in an "advisorial" capacity. It remained for the bravest and most foolish of them, a professor named Billy Graves, to undertake the benevolent supervision of the young firebrand from the sticks.

Billy was portly and blue-eyed and grey-haired, much beloved by women's clubs everywhere as a speaker. My aunts were charmed that such a well-known figure would take an interest in their nephew—dinners out, symphonies, auto trips, gifts of handsomely bound volumes of poesy, postcards and letters from England whither he went every summer—even coming to our modest house for a chicken dinner, and improvising brilliantly on our old upright piano.

Unfortunately I came to be more and more scornful of Billy's old-maid quality as my "sophistication" increased. He was not a practicing homosexual with me (nor I doubt with any one), and our only "romantic encounter" was my sleeping in the same bed with him one night while he caressed my back and shoulders. We drew gradually apart, and much later I heard that one of his fraternity brothers (he was Beta Theta Pi) took a swing at him for an attempted caress; then an obsessed female graduate student began to chase him everywhere, even to the door of the men's room. After some years, like a sad old Ulysses, he ended the pursuit by marrying the woman, and thereupon retired.

One day Marie Anderson, my huge lesbian friend, said to me: "M'dear, you really ought to take a course from Claire Andrews. He's teaching a survey this fall, and he rarely has anything open to sophomores. I'm taking it—why don't you? He's the best there is. No one on the whole damned campus can approach him."

Marie was right. I was fascinated by him from the first. He was a slim elegant man reminding me of Edwin Arlington Robinson's "Richard Cory," who "glittered when he walked." Always perfectly groomed, wearing glasses with narrow horn rims, with tie neatly knotted beneath a carefully trimmed mustache, he was the very model of the cosmopolite professor. He taught for six months of every year and then for the other six would disappear into the darkly romantic life of Paris, which he loved, and where he attended Gertrude Stein's salon many times. He had written several texts, and currently was enjoying the popularity brought to him by his book *The Innocents of Paris,* an extended love-song to the city and the vehicle for Maurice Chevalier's first American movie.

Andrews was infinitely more discreet than Billy Graves, and besides, he lived with a youngish painter named David Snodgrass who took care of his needs. I tried all my wiles but I could not penetrate Andrews' barrier. He often asked three or four students to his house to meet a visiting luminary—Yeats, Untermeyer, and others—and would serve sherry. But I could never get closer than that.

There were no secrets skipped over in his classes. He was the first I knew to speak openly about Oscar Wilde, the decadents of the 1890s, Byron, Shelley, and the rest. His lectures were scrupulously planned and impeccable jewels of organization, filled with bon mots and esoteric wordplays, and sometimes the dubious luxury of a high-level pun.

When he died of pneumonia on December 12, 1932 (that for all these years I should remember the exact date may indicate his effect on me), my world was darkened—even shattered. And it does not make me particularly happy to remember that six months after his death David Snodgrass got in touch with me. He had sold the house in Arlington and was living in a shabby section of Columbus. He had disposed of most of Andrews' valuable library but said that he wanted to return to me the copy of *Pan and the Firebird,* the short stories I had done in Andrews' class, which had been published. I had inscribed Andrews' copy in French to the "dear father of these stories."

Snodgrass got me drunk on gin and then crowed at me:

"And I suppose that all the time you thought your sainted Claire Andrews was above such low sins of the flesh! Well, let me tell you, dearie—he liked a good fuck as much as anyone, more so I expect, and I was just the one to ram it to him!"

He seized on me with a wide monkey-mouth, wet and smelling of liquor and onions, sucking at my lips with octopus-force, bruising them and making them bleed. He threw me on the narrow bunk bed and screwed me—and I endured it, thinking that the same cock which impaled me had been the one to bring pleasure to Andrews, and was therefore tolerable—my last and only link with my dead idol.

Snodgrass died about six months later of pneumonia, and left me wondering what had become of Emily Dickinson's amethyst cross, which Andrews had owned. Only one of the faculty went to the funeral.

All of the events of the early years at the university were turned even more dramatic by the fact that we were living in the 1920s, the Age of Discovery, and things were happening all around us that made life even more exciting. In a curious way, the 1920s were an *opening*, yet the primary struggle was against the forces which wanted to keep the period *closed*—puritanism and hypocrisy and optimism, the three-footed stool on which America rested. So we watched the birth of jazz and Dixieland, breaking the mold of Stephen Foster; we looked to our midsections as the glow from Freud filtered down to illuminate our crotches; we struggled against censorship—powerful forces under Anthony Comstock and the New York Society for the Suppression of Vice. We hunched over our crystal radio sets, fiddling with the cat-whisker to try to tease some night-music from the star-crackle and the static; we drank bathtub gin and homemade red wine. We read Dreiser and Anderson and Hemingway, sat through endless hours of O'Neill's tragedies, read smuggled copies of Joyce's *Ulysses*, adored Garbo and Stravinsky, listened in awe to the first "talkies," cheered Lindbergh's flight, and wept with the beauty of the Ballets Russes de Monte Carlo.

Going through the university meant some hard work for me. For a while I played piano with a "jazz band," the 1920s equivalent of today's combo or group, at fraternity dances.

Then I got a job in the library stacks, and over some years moved upwards until I had charge of the graduate seminar rooms in the library, nearly getting fired because a janitor once complained there were too many rubbers on the library steps every Saturday morning; they could have come only from the third floor where I presided. Ben Musser helped some financially, getting a rich old New York widow-woman to subsidize me with $300 once a year—and finally fellowships of the same value began to come my way. Thus I was able through all the years to pay part of my board and room.

My aunts' house on Seventeenth Avenue had about eleven rooms. In those years it held the aunts—now reduced to two: Minnie, the thin-lipped puritan one, disapproving of almost everything I did; and Elizabeth, whom we called Bebe, the quavery one, my favorite, who never disapproved of anything. The house held my sister Virginia also, five years younger than I. It fell to me to help guide her through the pits of sex, since the aunts knew nothing of it except menstruation. I enlightened her about the Facts of Life, telling her in the process that I considered myself homosexual until something better came along.

Six of the rooms were rented to two boys each, making a full house of a dozen young men. Over the years I managed to have about half the population of the place—some reluctant, some returning again and again.

A tennis star named Fred, clicking his bridge nervously with his tongue: "I'll give you just 'til I count ten, and if you ain't down on it by then you can't have it."

A farmboy named David from Delaware: "Hot damn! this's got a calf's mouth beat all holler!"

A Polish boy from Cleveland: "Go ahead—I don't think I gotta confess this."

Julius, unbuttoning his shirt: "I've read that book you wrote, and I've got something for you."

Dick, from New York: "I always pay for it—you take the two bucks and buy a book."

Hal, from Cincinnati: "You sure you ain't gonna tell anybody?"

Don, from Germantown: "You got a tighter asshole than

Clyde has by far."

Lloyd: "Get away! You're lucky I don't tell your aunts and move out."

Eddie (peeking around my door at four a.m.): "My gal's on the rag—kin I come in for a while?"

Such were some of the *divertissements* that helped to enliven the study of Anglo-Saxon grammar. Anything that was new was tried. It was not only the Age of Discovery but of Experimentation as well.

Even before I had left Woodsfield there were signs of rebellion in me, of a loathing for authority and taking orders; yet with another side of me, I loved taking orders. Much depended, I suppose, on the origin of the commands. Authority in general, in its largest aspects, made me want to revolt against it—a kind of "Imp of the Perverse" reaction. But a command, such as the one from Fred, the tennis player, was relished and obeyed with alacrity.

In Columbus at the university the stubbornness often surfaced. There was the question of pledging fraternities, for example. Towards the end of my freshman year, I was solicited by the "Dekes" up the Seventeenth Avenue ravine. Their house had a roughhewn stone facade and some amber-glass windows that evidently reminded me of Camelot and my early reading of King Arthur stories. The Dekes needed brains to pull up their point averages, and someone had evidently been following my grades. I was also impressed, on my first tour through their house, by an uproarious gang of burly handsome athletes in a room, watching one of their number—an Apollo with his pants and underwear off, legs lifted high as he rested on a bed with his back against the wall, while an assistant with matches lighted his prodigious farts, which shot like the blasts from a small flamethrower out into the room. I pledged almost at once.

But once theirs, I didn't like it. Fraternity snobbishness was foreign to me, for I was in love with a) physical beauty joined to b) brains, and c) my own independence. Orders from the mindless hulks of brothers turned annoying, and I stopped waxing floors in the house. The pledge-master threatened me; I excused myself because of the work in the library and

having to keep my grades high. So I pledged another fraternity on another street, because I was assured their demands
were nearly nonexistent.

The only difficulty was that I pledged while still a Deke.

I soon heard from the Dean of Men. "What do you mean by
joining two fraternities at the same time?"

I shrugged. "It enlarges my outlook," I said.

"This is unheard of," he stormed. "Your membership in
both is cancelled."

Cancelled—and ever thereafter blackballed! Alas!

Marie Anderson thought the action delicious; Robert von
Riegel roared with laughter. Claire Andrews learned of it
when I entered his class a year later, and congratulated me on
my "fresh and innovative approach to campus politics."

Another protest movement I started came to a sudden end. I
thought it would be nice for all sororities and fraternities to be
"integrated"—the word did not yet exist in its current sense
so I phrased it: "opened to all races and creeds."

That got me another interview with the Dean of Men who
called me a troublemaker, and suggested that I would do
better at another university unless I mended my ways. Since
the Crash had just occurred, I decided to stop my "liberating"
crusades.

But the worst of my protests, before I stopped them, involved the ROTC—compulsory military training in a land-
grant college. Most of the students hated ROTC with a
passion. I talked a guy named Lloyd into a silly plan of protest, conceived with the typical and reasonable unreason of
sophomores, of stealing a rifle a day and hiding them, gradually throwing them into the Olentangy River until they were
all gone.

We got caught by the campus cop on the very first heist. He
turned us loose, but President Rightmire wanted to see us. His
letter ruined the summer vacation for both Lloyd and me. In
the fall when the dreaded second of October arrived, two
white-faced and visibly trembling young men sat stickily on
the leather divan in the President's waiting room.

Then came our turn, into the wood-paneled office.

"Sit down," said the President, looking stern. "What am I to do with you?" He turned to me. "Mr. Steward—just what was your purpose in attempting to steal that rifle? Did you intend to sell it?"

"Oh, n-no, sir," I said, shaken by the direct attack. "I wouldn't have known how to or where."

"Are you that much in need of money?" he asked.

"N-no, sir," I said. "I w-work in the library, and although I don't have any to waste I am managing to get along."

President Rightmire turned to Lloyd. "And you?"

Lloyd turned fire-red. "My-my father can afford to send me to college, sir."

Back to me. "Then why in the world did you do it?"

I plunged. "It was a thoughtless gesture, sir," I said. "And I am entirely responsible for it. Lloyd came along just because I talked him into it. But I hated ROTC training so much—and have for two years—and I despise everything it stands for, that I was going to throw the rifle into the river, along with as many others as I could manage."

The white tufted eyebrows went up. "You weren't planning to profit in any way from this?"

"No-no, sir," I said. I could feel my ears flaming. I looked wide-eyed at him.

"And you did it just because you disapprove of ROTC training?"

"Y-yessir," I gulped.

He fiddled with a pen on his desk and then looked at us.

"Well, so do I," he said, breaking into a wide grin. "But I'm here to enforce the laws of the state and the university as a land-grant college, and I can't do anything about it."

I could not believe what I was hearing.

He continued to smile. "And if either of you says a word about this or quotes me in any way, I'll see to it that you really are expelled. And of course I'll deny that I said any such thing. Now," he said, standing up behind his desk, "get out of here, both of you, and don't let me ever see you again until I hand you your diplomas."

And life went on. I grew more discreet about adventuring—or at least taking part in episodes which endangered my university life.

One of my best friends on campus, who introduced me to the nonacademic bohemian crowd of Columbus, was my huge friend, J. Marie Anderson. She had swooped down on me one day and made me her own.

Marie was not a girl to go unnoticed. She was tall, about five-nine, and heavy, about two hundred. For all her size she moved with a swirl and a gazelle's grace. She had bright yellow hair in a longish bob which curled and swayed and swept back from her face. Her thin penciled eyebrows were more active than swallows, darting up and down, each separately controlled. Her short nose was well-formed and her full mobile lips always painted the most vivid scarlet. She accentuated her bulk by wearing a capelike overgarment with sleeve-slits. Through her I met Robert von Riegel, a flamboyant sandy-haired actor-type who was always on stage. He had wanted to meet me, he said, because I looked as if I always spent my afternoons dipping yellow ladyfingers into purple tea.

Marie was a true lesbian. She was in love with a rather plain and pleasant girl named Alice, but her real passion was Garbo, whom she sketched endlessly in charcoal.

"You must come with me down to Long Street," she said one day.

"What on earth for?" It was a dismal part of town, close to the bus station.

"Because," said Marie.

"A woman's answer," I said, a reply calculated to annoy her.

"There's an old building at number 31," she said, "three-story, an absolute honeycomb, m'dear, of small apartments and studios. Our very own Bohemia."

I'd been reading Ben Hecht's *Count Bruga*, and knew all about Greenwich Village. I went with her.

It was an old evil-smelling building—disinfectant, mold, and stale urine—with twisted crazy stairways, a rabbit-warren of rooms and hallways, very confusing. The calcimine flaked from the walls and unshaded light bulbs dangled from ceiling cords like strangled felons. Their feeble light made our shadows grotesque on the walls.

26

So I met Jon Gillespie, artiste, eating his evening meal of two small wieners atop a shredded wheat biscuit. He had sunken pale eyes, high cheekbones and hollow cheeks, and pale lank hair. He was in love with Russell Griffin, a square-jawed handsome blond giant down the hall, who painted (but not very well), and who introduced us to the music of Erik Satie.

Russell in turn was in love with Tee Walley, a charming large-nosed intellectual girl who had to do with Russell, as well as with this or that girlfriend. Permissiveness was by no means invented in the 1960s; it was with us early.

Below Jon and Russell lived Bobby Creighton, who was very free with her body. She had a short frizzy bob of yellow black-rooted hair. Bobby entertained her guests either in see-through negligee or in nothing at all. Her library was fantastic for those times, and she lent me many esoteric items—the early poetry of Pound, of Joyce and Stein and e.e.cummings, the suppressed drawings of Beardsley for *Lysistrata*, the writing of Ronald Firbank, the drawings of Félicien Rops, the work of J. K. Huysmans (*Against the Grain* and *Down There*) and many others. My education bounded ahead.

Once Marie introduced me to this charmed circle, I was there in all the free time I could find. I was so much a part of the circle, indeed, that once I went with Bobby to Lima, Ohio, to visit someone, and remember waking up in bed with her and a handsome young man (she had slept between us) who was slowly, leisurely screwing her in the morning and paying no attention to me whatsoever. I caressed his moving buttocks and made him mad.

T. C. Wilson, Ted, was a published poet, a shy dark little boy; if he were homosexual he was deeply in the closet. But he was an intimate friend of Benjamin Musser, Poet Laureate of New Jersey. I knew Ohio's Poet Laureate, Tessa Sweazy Webb—who once invited me downtown to hear Benjamin Musser read his poems. I arrived late with a torn knee in my trouser-leg (an accident with a streetcar) and was forced to sit in the front row. Ben—as he later said—could not take his eyes from the rip nor from my "ethereal face."

And lo! from that chance meeting (as Huysmans wrote in *A Rebours*) there sprang a mistrustful friendship that endured for several years.

Ben was married to a fairly wealthy woman—and he sent me money. He also paid for several roundtrips to Atlantic City where he lived, and for the first time in my life I flew in an airplane, TAT (Transcontinental Air Transport, later to become TWA), from Columbus to Philadelphia. One such trip through a thunderstorm was memorable; we flew just under the cloud-line, out of which jagged flashes burst alarmingly near. And the plane was not weatherproof. It leaked directly over my seat; the nurse gave me a tarpaulin. The meal was a cheese sandwich in waxed paper. You had a pioneer's feeling, doing a daredevil thing. You felt like Lindbergh who had flown the Atlantic in 1927, only two years before.

Ben published a poem or two of mine in his magazine *Contemporary Verse*, and in 1930 subsidized the publication of a volume of my short sketches and stories, *Pan and the Firebird*, done in Andrews' writing class. Ben's introduction was extravagant; he called me the golden boy, heir to Theocritus, and said he had known me twenty-five hundred years ago when I was "an engrossing young Greek." Then he confused matters by additionally calling me a "gorgeous Renaissance personality."

But our eternal love could not endure. He was forty, I was twenty. We gradually drifted apart as graduate studies and research took more and more of my time.

With Andrews gone, the mentor's mantle passed to Harlan Hatcher in the English department—perhaps as brilliant as Andrews but with a quieter personality. Around him swirled as many legends and as much fog as had around Andrews. He had been, it was said, a Kaintucky mountain boy who showed up barefoot at a tiny Ohio college in a raggedy Huck Finn costume—astounding everyone by his intelligence and the way he sailed through college.

It was nonsense, of course. He had a perfectly ordinary middle-class background. I did my master's thesis under him, and then my doctoral dissertation on Newman's Oxford Movement and its connection with literary romanticism. It was a heluva long thing enlivened mainly by the fact that I discovered John Henry Newman to have been a homosexual, who had even asked to be buried (and was) in the same grave with his friend Ambrose St. John, and who had the walls of his private chapel covered with pictures of his male friends instead of saints.

Such a little tidbit, released on a faculty committee in 1934, was almost as much a bombshell as my early essay on Whitman. Jesuits outside the university complained about it.

The trouble was that about two years previously I had become a Catholic—a gesture of rebellion again, and part of the Age of Experimentation. I was not yet perfectly adjusted; I needed crutches to lean on, as Marie said. She tried to get me to use her crutch—the Communist party, then very chic—but I couldn't because I had seen her lose her sense of humor when she was "converted."

I went into the church by the back door. First of all I read in Wilde's *The Picture of Dorian Gray* about a book in which "in exquisite raiment, and to the delicate sound of flutes the sins of the world were passing in dumb show before him," a book filled with "metaphors as monstrous as orchids," a "poisonous" book about strange purple sins.

The book was Huysmans' *Against the Grain.* Its sensuality and erudition fascinated me, enchanted me, for it described the life of the senses in terms of mystical philosophy. The exploits of its anti-hero, Des Esseintes, seemed to range from the ecstasies of a medieval saint to the confessions of a modern sensualist and sinner.

That was the first step. The second was taking a course in the Reformation under a sly and witty history professor whose innuendos and crafty indictments of the Catholic Church called up the imp of the perverse in me once again, and made me stubbornly determined to find out more about Catholicism.

How richly colorful the vestments of the church seemed when I first attended a mass! Romantic that I was, the panoply, the incense, the Latin—all worked a spell on me. Browning's bishop of St. Praxed's affected me deeply with images like:

>   . . . I shall lie through centuries,
> And hear the blessed mutter of the mass,
> And see God made and eaten all day long,
> And feel the steady candle-flame, and taste
> Good strong thick stupefying incense-smoke!

Then, having developed a passionate admiration for Huysmans, I read *Down There*, a study of Satanism and the Black Mass in Paris. Drawn ever deeper into the writings of the French aesthete, I went with him on his climb back from atheism to the Church in *En Route, The Cathedral,* and finally *The Oblate.*

That did it. By the time I had fully absorbed Huysmans, I was a Catholic. And this strange odd period of stop-and-go celibacy and sin lasted for a year and a half.

President Rightmire solemnly winked at me when he bestowed on me the scarlet and grey hood of my doctorate in 1934, and handed me my diploma. I was now ready to go out into the world to bring light and culture and English grammar to mankind.

Chapter III

OUT OF THE NURSERY,
INTO THE WIDE WIDE

I N JUNE, 1934, THE DEPRESSION was nearly five years old, and you took what job you could get. A college placement office called me shortly after graduation. There was an opening for the summer session at Davis and Elkins College. (Where in heaven's name was that? Oh, in Elkins, West Virginia . . .)

"Are you available?"

"Yes, indeed," and off I went. It was like going back to Woodsfield—perhaps worse. In Ohio I had grown up gradually with the narrow attitudes, becoming somewhat hardened to them. Then came the freedom of Columbus. But in Elkins I was suddenly thrust deep into bigotry once again after the comparative liberalism of the university.

The President of the college was a born Christian, Presbyterian subgenus. No need to call him "born again"; he had never lost it. The original cramped mold still held him together. His wife was a First Families of Virginia old broad named Parke. She was one of the first women to find me "motherable," as Gertrude Stein was later to say. Parke served me wine and liquor, although the *mores* of the town and of her husband made it necessary to keep it all secret.

The two of them rattled around in a decaying ghostly gothic mansion called Halliehurst. It was all of sagging wood with a creaking two-story porch running halfway around it. Inside there was an echoing wood-paneled dining room with a long table that could have seated thirty. Hollywood might have used it for a horror film.

It was an odd time. I lived "downtown" at the YMCA, which that summer was filled with earnest young Mormon missionaries bent on proselytizing anyone who would pause, and I often found time to listen, especially to the handsomest ones, whose scorn of the human body was such that they frequently went to and from the showers draped only in a scanty YMCA towel. Although they talked long and solemnly about "secret abominations" and the "abominable connections" of man and woman, and of "works in darkness," these young zealots seemed genuinely fascinated by the evil stalking the corridors in the person of the young sinner who taught at the wicked college up the hill. Several of them sinned repeatedly with this ungodly man.

The students of that summer session were mostly sincere females bent on acquiring a B.A. so they could teach in the highschools of the state. One of my courses was the tragedies of Shakespeare.

A sample of education in Elkins: I was one day endeavoring to explain in delicate terms the meaning of "cuckold" when a lank-haired, flat-heeled, bespectacled pimply girl in the front row said:

"Doctor Steward, does that word mean the same as 'w-h-o-r-e' that I see a lot in Shakespeare?"

Try to get out of that one. I ignored the greasy sniggers from the boys in the back row. "No," said I, "that word *may* refer to the wife who makes a cuckold of her husband," and fled to the next topic.

In Elkins I became acquainted with the Catholic Vicar Apostolic, raised in rank and power above an ordinary priest, in order to deal with the inbreeding and interfamily copulations (for there were no marriages) of the savages living in remote regions of Appalachia. His tales of how to approach these half-human beasts—naked, cowering in lean-tos and sheltered in caves, gnawing on bloody uncooked meat on carpets of bones amid unbelievable stench—were fascinating and hair-raising. The fornications of mother and son, brother and sister, and father and daughter had produced things that were less than noble, and the Vicar had to try to straighten it all out.

One night the college dean invited a group of us to dinner and afterwards we talked a lot, sitting on the porch swing and in rocking chairs with the smell of honeysuckle strong in the twilight air, and the swing-chains squeaking near the ceiling.

The conversation shifted to religion. I sensed that I was being evaluated, considered for a full-time winter job. Each of us expressed himself or herself in some way about God's salvation and the beauties of fundamentalist Christianity. Then one of them fell to damning the Vicar Apostolic for interfering in "the folkways of the mountain people." That led to a genuine Woodsfieldian burst of misinformation about guns in Catholic basements, the secret tunnels, the scarlet women dressed as nuns, and on and on.

During this time I was quite silent, and finally the dean in his oily Presbyterian tones with the minor-third inflection at each sentence-end said, "And what faith do you profess, Doctor Steward?"

"Well," I said, "after investigating a great number of faiths and considering the historical evidence carefully, I was forced to conclude there was only one uninterrupted religion which could be traced back to Jesus, and so about six months ago I joined the Holy Roman Catholic Church."

The silence was profound. The porch swing stopped squeaking. A mosquito sang above our heads, and my wicker rocker went noisily on.

Finally the Dean spoke. "Interesting," he said, "and I am glad we live in a day when all faiths can commingle."

I got no offer for the fall term.

"Why in the world did you have to tell them that?" Parke scolded me angrily.

I shrugged. "Despite your pleasant company," I said, "a year in Elkins would drive me completely mad."

When I returned to Columbus there was word from the placement agency of an opening in a small college in Helena, Montana. It sounded awful—$100 a month, room and board, a dormitory Catholic college called Carroll—but it would cut the umbilical cord that had until then bound me close to aunts and family.

And the West! The glamorous unspoiled West! Cowboys! The gold rush! Chaps! Ghost towns! Cowboys! Silver and gold mines! Cowboys! Ah, I would like the West!

I did not, particularly. Trying to teach cowboys and the sons of cowboys about semicolons is not a rewarding pastime. There was nothing to do in the Helena evenings except play chess and look at the Rocky Mountains twenty miles away, blue, serene, and cloud-capped. A few friends were made, and there were Sunday afternoon drives of three hundred miles or more—to see ghost towns, abandoned gold mines, hangman's trees, tumbleweeds, and haystacks that cured green inside. There were no dollar bills—only silver dollars in change, that wore a hole in your pocket very quickly. And it got cold! That winter there were three weeks of minus 35° weather, which warmed up to −30° in the afternoons; if you went outside your face had to be swathed and your kneecaps wrapped. We amused ourselves by spitting or thinly pouring a glass of water from the third-floor window; by the time it hit the ground it tinkled and shattered—ice.

Almost every evening I would be tanked on sherry, for my life as an alcoholic was by now well under way. To my barren room with its institutionally-colored green and buff walls I would invite some favorite students—picking out those I perceived were "club-members" or soon would be. Jimmy and Gerry were inseparable; I was not sure about Sherman; Juan would screw anything that was circular or would fit him.

Juan always washed out his rubbers and used them again. One night, drunk, we went to Ida's, the reigning whorehouse in Helena—the only one I ever saw with a neon sign: "Ida's. Rooms *With* Girls." Juan went upstairs whilst I sat and talked with Ida, who could make or break any new shop which opened in Helena. A floral wreath with a banner saying "From Ida and the Girls" was prominently displayed in those new shop windows which made the grade.

My departure from the Church began in Helena. Not only did a couple of priests try to make me (horrible experience for a new convert), but when I went to confession I was disturbed to see the priest pop out of the confessional to see who had confessed such lurid sins. And then there was a tremendous guilt feeling, caused by my getting drunk one night and slipping into the bed of a redheaded cowboy I had found

34

sexually exciting; undoubtedly he confessed his sin, and named his partner.

For three years I had been corresponding with Gertrude Stein, having written to her about the death of Claire Andrews, who had so often visited her salon. She had responded warmly, and our letter-writing continued. When she and Alice made their whirlwind trip through America in 1934-35, lecturing at colleges and clubs, I tried to arrange for her to come to Helena. But the state universities of Montana, Oregon, and Washington—isolated from what was going on in literature—did not know enough about her to invite her to speak under their auspices, and Gertrude and Alice sailed back to France. My broken heart was partly mended when Gertrude sent me a large matted Van Vechten photograph of herself with a considerable message written on the mat.

To end this miserable year, I wrote an article for a national Catholic magazine on the "lay faculty" and the shabby treatment given them—a youthful blast against the priests who thought the laying on of hands gave them the wisdom to teach mathematics or sociology. In it I complained bitterly about the insults and humiliations which turned the lay teacher into a kind of "glorified janitor."

All hell, you might say, broke loose.

The article stirred up loud, resentful, caustic, and sour discussions in the faculty room—and also in the pages of the magazine where the argument raged for many issues, until—as the editor said—the quarrel was "called on account of darkness."

I left Carroll without asking to return, having secured a position for fall at the State College of Washington at Pullman.

But there was still the summer to fill. I became information clerk, selling packsaddle trips at Lake McDonald Hotel at the west end of Glacier Park.

The surroundings were serene. Mornings and afternoons you could watch the fantastic play of light on the mountain range called the Garden Wall, and as evening came see it blaze with scarlet, then change to darkest purple and finally fade into the black of night. The sky produced lovely orgies of wildest magenta, topaz, and garnet—and even on sunless days turned the mountains grey and silver, shimmering in the green-black waters of the lake. In the chalet the fire burned every evening, in a fireplace large enough to sit inside on rough log benches. And it was fun to try to make the tall grey-eyed butch bellboy, whose last name was Bull.

It was all my own little kingdom for a while, until brash young handsome Clayton burst like a small whirlwind onto the scene. He was loud and bossy; we didn't get along. It was a classic case of personality clash, which eventually turned into backstabbing as the summer went on. The whole hotel was aware of our feud, although it was a quiet one with no loud arguing.

One of the major difficulties was that we had to room together in a very small log cabin. The other was that physically Clayton was very attractive to me—a heavy sexual aura, extremely handsome with black curly hair, and a body with excellently-defined musculature. Watching him undress from my lower bunk bed created both temptation and desire in me. And one evening when there was a dance in one of the buildings, Clayton broke all the rules, got drunk and danced with the "dudes," and was put off the floor.

I was in bed when he came to the cabin drunk much later, and had to help him get undressed. It was too much for me. He could not climb up into his own bunk, so he slept in mine—and so did I, moving to the upper one in the early dawn. Put another card into my Stud File.

The next day Clayton went to the manager and accused me of making homosexual advances to him, and the manager called me in. She was a tiny grandmotherly woman with white hair. She told me what he had said.

I sputtered with histrionic outrage. She silenced me with her hand.

"It's nonsense, I know," she said. "Anyone who has watched you two squabble all summer would know that homosexual advances would be the last thing you would make. Clayton was drunk and obnoxious, and I have already asked him to leave. Why don't you ask Bull to be there while he packs?"

36

I did—and Clayton left, furious. Bull moved into the cabin, and the rest of the summer was very interesting indeed.

When fall arrived I went on to the State College of Washington at Pullman. I liked the ambience—the rolling green hills intensely emerald from the abundant rain and snowfall, a real Grant Wood landscape. And I also liked the idea of teaching in a state school, away from the religiosity of places like Carroll and Davis and Elkins. But Washington, alas, was not as free and intellectual as one might think. The narrow ideas of the other places were still there—differently and subtly rearranged. Consider the question of alcohol. In Washington you had to purchase a permit before you could buy liquor. President Holland did not approve of liquor. He tried to compel the state licensing board to reveal which faculty members had purchased permits, threatening to fire everyone who imbibed the Demon Rum. He did not get the list, or I would have been out before I started.

There really was not much more life in Pullman outside the college than there had been in Helena. The faculty was extremely dull, inbred, and disastrously gossipy. I had a few friends but no intimate ones: an English teacher named Karl was a club-member, but as fussy an old-maid as one could imagine. There was a lot of time that year to fall in love a hundred times, and I was almost constantly enamored of the fine upstanding young heterosexual male students, the western ideal that I had seen suggestions of in Montana. They seemed taller and straighter and leaner and handsomer than midwesterners, and perhaps they actually were.

In the Housman manner I wrote scores of melancholy poems about handsome young men I couldn't have. It was a streak of extravagant masochism in me, I suppose, that made me "fall in love" time after time, be rejected, and therefore suffer—so that loving and suffering always seemed to go together. I felt I didn't deserve to be loved by any of the godlike idols I worshiped, and on the rare occasions when one stepped down from his pedestal to give even the slightest token of affection in return, I fled from such encounters startled and confused in alarm and dismay. This did not keep me, however, from having a considerable number of sexual releases with handsome young animals who were not gods but men.

Things were thus not unpleasant overall, and in March I was told that my contract would be renewed for another year.

The spring term was somewhat enlivened for me by reading the galleys for a novel that I had written while still at Ohio State. It was a campus novel titled *Angels on the Bough*, about a group of ten persons and the ways in which their lives were woven together. In essence it was close to Wilder's *The Bridge of San Luis Rey*, for it gently presented the question of whether things happen by accident or design, and just as wisely as Wilder's novel it failed to give any definite answer. The book was scheduled for appearance in May.

But in April something else happened. For some time there had been campus rumblings and rumors about a new set of "rules" of campus conduct to be released. They were finally made public and the uproar began, for the rules were insulting to the students, presupposing evil sexual intent on everyone's part. Samples: No pillows to be allowed on picnics. No alcoholic beverages of any kind to be permitted in fraternity or sorority houses. Any student possessing a contraceptive device to be dismissed immediately. All girls to be in their residences no later than ten on weeknights and eleven on weekends. If in an auto a girl rides on a boy's lap there had to be four thicknesses of blanket between.

This was too much for the students even in 1936, and we were witness to one of the first student strikes ever held in the United States. The young people refused to go to classes.

I was delighted with their actions and said so to the many student friends who kept tramping up to my quarters to ask advice on this or that. I was careful to be cautionary in my advice, being aware of Holland's spy network. Only to a few treasured ones did I say "Go ahead and strike, damnit! It's time for some common sense around here."

The strike was ended in two days; the rules were withdrawn, and the students won.

The day after commencement, when all the students had gone home, a call came from the President's office, ordering me to a conference. The dean and the department head were there.

"Sit down, Steward," said President Holland. "I'll get right to the point. I understand although I have not yet read it that you have written a racy novel with a streetwalker in it."

My mouth fell open. He went on.

"Such a thing brings discredit to the college and its faculty, and we cannot have that," the craggy old sonofabitch continued. "Accordingly, your connection with the university is terminated, and your contract declared null and void."

I know that I turned white. "B-but Professor Bundy and Dean Todd said—"I began.

"I don't care what they said. They have nothing to do with it. I say you are terminated and that is final. You may all now leave."

We filed out. I was in shock. Bundy, the department head, attempted to pat my shoulder.

"Don't touch me, you damned hypocrite!" I shouted. "Both you and Todd are milksops!"

I fled the building, shaking with rage.

Luckily I belonged to the American Association of University Professors, and after making a formal complaint to them and waiting a few months, I was gratified to read their published report censuring Holland, and criticizing the administration for "tending to make barren college and university departments of English," holding that a teacher who is a creative writer should have complete freedom of expression so long as his output does not conflict with postal or other laws, and saying that Holland's handling of my case was ill-judged, indicating bad conditions of academic tenure and improper restriction of literary freedom.

The membership of the AAUP in Pullman, up to that time a meager twenty-five or so, jumped to over four hundred the following year.

Meanwhile, an opening was announced at Loyola University in Chicago. I hardly wanted to go back into religious teaching, but I sent a copy of my novel to the dean there, explaining all. He found it innocuous, and I was hired, to teach in an English department under the direction of Morton

Dauwen Zabel, one of the most feared and respected scholars in the field.

When I first arrived in Chicago, I hated its filth—the squalor of the south side tenements, the mud of the back-yards, the dirt of its gutters—all in contrast with the gleaming lakefront and the bright shops of Michigan Avenue. The paradox of State Street astounded me—beginning in nothing-ness at the river, running a few blocks down through the proud stores ... into what? You crossed Van Buren, and were in a skidrow of tattoo joints, burlesque houses, prostitutes, winos, and flophouses.

Gradually, however, I came to think of Chicago as a man-city, healthy, sweaty, and sensual. It was Gargantua of the lake front—his head in Evanston, his feet in Gary; and he lay relaxed and smoldering along the water. The trees of Lincoln Park were the curling man-hair of his chest, the trees of Jackson Park the foliage on his legs, the tall buildings of the Loop his sturdy upstanding phallus—the whole anatomy of the city his outstretched body.

I really learned to love the place. I spent time wandering—watching the lights of the tall buildings around Wacker Drive break and glitter in the water. The lake at midnight was sometimes wild and blowing, with the air full of King Lear. I would stand on an embankment overlooking darkness and see no line between sky and water, only a sullen noisy void with whiteness fretting and circling at my feet and a coiling black film of water sweeping over a sanded beach, ending finally in a thin and crisping edge of foam.

Once again I began to like teaching, too, although Zabel worked us unmercifully. His razor mind under his youthfully bald pate made him the archetypal egghead, with a soft voice that could cut like a blade of Toledo steel if necessary. Although he was a taskmaster, everyone was comparatively free under him. Did the schedule call for a course in the modern novel? *All right, Doctor Steward, will you teach it?* Delighted—but what about modern novelists in this religious school? *Please forget about that—the modern novel is the modern novel, of course.* Won't they expect one to teach novelists like Belloc and Chesterton? *Of course not—include*

40

anyone you want. Dreiser? Hemingway? Anderson? Lewis? *Certainly—they are modern novelists, aren't they?*

Zabel turned me into a better scholar than I had ever been before. A perfectionist himself, he expected it in others. He was a talented and meticulous savant with an encyclopedic mind, a giant of learning. How such a university managed to keep him remained a mystery, although eventually he went to the University of Chicago where he belonged from the beginning.

There were many friends made in Chicago over the quarter-century I lived there. On my first trip to Europe, a literary pilgrimage, Gertrude Stein gave me the names of Wendell and Esther Wilcox, who belonged to one of the many intellectual circles revolving around the University of Chicago. Theirs included Gertrude Abercrombie and Charles Sebree, artists; Thornton Wilder and Fritz Leiber, writers—and others.

I had not been in Chicago long when I was propositioned on an elevated platform by a white-faced, heavily beardmarked flabby sort of gentleman in his mid-forties. I was then twenty-seven. I avoided him by giving a phony telephone number— but he waylaid me again on the same platform.

"You must come over some evening for dinner. I'm staying with some charming people."

And that was how I met Emmy Curtis and her mother. The man's name was Harry Winthrop. Emmy was to have a profound effect on my life. At the beginning I exercised my usual casual attitude towards women with her; she seemed no threat to me, for she was obviously in love with Harry. She had been married, but had little experience at it for her husband died early. She was eighteen years older than I.

Harry was making good use of her and her mother. He existed on some sort of meager pension and was always broke. He freeloaded on them, staying in their apartment for a month-long stopover on the way from Wisconsin to Florida. He borrowed large sums from Emmy and never repaid them, always leading Emmy to think that he would marry her "as soon as my ship comes in."

As my fondness for Emmy and her mother developed over

the years, I grew more and more irritated with the double game Winthrop played, and felt that I had to interfere. Accordingly, one evening after I had fortified myself with several old-fashioneds, I let fly.

"Do you know, m'dear," I said, "that Harry Winthrop is queer?"

"He certainly does have a lot of strange ways," said Emmy, laughing.

"I'll have to explain," I said. "Harry likes men only. Not women. If you're thinking he'll marry you, better get over it. He's just using you and your home as a stopover on the way to Florida."

Having gone that far, and bedeviled by my Methodist honesty, I knew I had to continue. "I can't tell you this without saying that I'm also homosexual. Harry 'cruised' me on the El platform. I will also tell you that we have never had any sexual encounters."

I was not watching her while I said these things, and I felt like a Judas. When I looked at her again she had lowered her face and was weeping soundlessly into a small square of handkerchief. Her pain was contagious; my own eyes filled.

"I'm sorry," I said, "but I couldn't stand to see you and your mother made fools of, nor you to go on hoping that some day you'd be married to him."

When she stopped crying, she said, "I've been an idiot. I knew something was wrong, especially when he seemed to be in trouble and begged me not to answer the phone, and to deny I knew anyone named Winthrop."

Emmy recovered, but before long I noticed a change—a subtle "rebound" or "transference" reaction so beloved by psychiatrists. She sliced Winthrop out of her life, and replaced him with me. Years later we started to go to bed together. She was a dear and faithful friend, going with me in 1950 to Paris to see Alice Toklas. It was there that the first signs of the mysterious ailment appeared which took her life: at a restaurant I was horrified to see this gentle well-bred grey-haired woman try to eat peas with her knife. It was the beginning of polycythemia, in which the red blood thickens, clogs the capillaries, and impedes the brain's functioning. I

42

joked with her as much as possible—called her Lady Macbeth who cried "Make thick my blood!" and went with her when she had to drink radioactive phosphorus to control the raging enemy within her veins, asking if her urine now glowed in the dark . . . And as the disease grew steadily worse for ten years and could no longer be controlled, I acted as her court-appointed conservator, seeing her into a nursing home, watching her waste away until her hands were mere claws at the end of scrawny flesh-covered bones, weaving and weaving in the air, calling for me . . . And with the tears flowing, holding her befouled fingers, I listened to the long-dammed stream of ugly words issuing from her proper lips. Finally, from this nest of stink and foulness her spirit was released, and the struggle was over.

Then the vultures descended, the distant relatives who had abandoned her in her illness, tearing her apartment to pieces, looking for silverware, diamonds, antiques, no matter what; and Emmy was gone irrevocably, and with her the last vestige of sexual attraction that I ever felt for a woman.

Chapter IV

THE MAGIC SUMMER

S OMETIMES, LOOKING BACK OVER THE succession of
years in a life, it is possible to pick out a watershed, a
continental divide—and the summer of 1937 was that for
me.

The loosely bound group at Ohio State University which
embraced Marie Anderson, Robert von Riegel, Virginia
Cooley, myself and others considered itself in the
forefront—very sophisticated and au courant. Possibly we
were by those days' standards—maybe even intellectual
and avant-garde. Measured by today's we were only grop-
ing towards the kinds of esoteric knowledge that are old
hat, even corny, to the young of the moment.

Robert von Riegel's channel was dramatic; Marie's was
artistic; mine was literary. I had started the correspondence
with Gertrude Stein to inform her of Claire Andrews' death,
and her continuing letters put me just a notch above my
rivals. Such success had led me to write letters of appre-
ciation and flattery to many of the authors I admired. My
list of replies, expanding, came to include Thomas Mann,
Van Vechten, Cabell, Undset, Housman, Morley, O'Neill,
Freud, Yeats, Maugham, Gide, Rolland, and others. The
trick to getting a response, I found, was to say something
intelligent about an author's work, and *never to ask any*
questions nor ask for anything in my letters, not even a
reply. It worked.

TEA WITH LORD ALFRED

Naturally, whenever a literary figure came to the campus to
lecture, we were all there en masse—to hear John Cowper
Powys declaim like thunder, and James Stephens read

Keats in a murmurous whisper—and in 1934 to listen to Hamlin Garland, who wrote *A Son of the Middle Border*, give us the October reminiscences of his long career. He was a pleasant silver-haired giant, by then somewhat diminished in reputation and obscured by men like Hemingway and Dreiser and Sinclair Lewis. But during the course of his lecture he mentioned that he had known Whitman, and that electrified me.

Afterwards I went up on the stage to speak to him. "Did you really know Whitman?" I asked in awe.

"Yes," said the patriarch. "I was very young, but he shook my hand and laid his hand on top of my head."

"Well, Mr. Garland," I said with the rash bravado of youth, "I've shaken your hand, but may I put my hand where Whitman laid his?"

He was somewhat taken aback, but he smiled.

"I want to be linked in with Whitman," I stammered, feeling my face grow red.

"Of course," he said, and bowed his head slightly. I put my left hand on his silver mane. Someone giggled, and I escaped sweating into the auditorium.

That was the genesis of the idea. The next day I wrote to Lord Alfred Douglas, finding his address in *Who's Who*. And in due time a letter from him arrived, chatty and somewhat avuncular, asking who I was and telling me about his latest book, *The True History of Shakespeare's Sonnets*. I answered, saying that I was a student working on my doctorate, and that I would try to find a copy of his book somewhere in the States. He replied that he would be glad to send me a copy but he would have to charge me for it since all his author's copies had been given out. I sent him a draft for two pounds sterling, and waited.

The book arrived. It contained the "dedication" of a full page in his handwriting, with the statement that he had corrected two misprints.

It soon became obvious from his inquiries in letters that followed, inquiries that were at first veiled and then direct, that what Lord Alfred was really looking for was someone who could help him find an American publisher for *The True*

History; and I had to confess to him that I had no ties or any influence in the publishing world. And at that point our correspondence dwindled and died ...

... until three years later, 1937, when I made my first trip to Europe as a literary pilgrim, to visit Gertrude Stein at her invitation, and Thomas Mann and André Gide, all of whom seemed a little curious about me. And after a little side trip to Trinity College at Cambridge University to visit Whewell's Court and Great Court B2 where A. E. Housman had lived for twenty-five years (to stand silently weeping, with chills along my spine), I wrote again to Lord Alfred and received a short note from him, asking me to come down to Hove to call on him should I find the time during my London stay.

I must honestly admit that I had no interest whatsoever in Lord Alfred Douglas as a person or as a writer, but only in the fact that he and Oscar Wilde had been lovers, and that back in those shrouded days the name of Wilde had a magic all its own for us who had to live without the benefits of liberation or exposure of our wicked lives. Besides, I was in my twenties and Lord Alfred was by then sixty-seven, and in anyone's book that's *old*. To go to bed with him was hardly the most attractive prospect in the world—it was terrifying, even repulsive. But if I wanted to link myself to Oscar Wilde more directly than I was linked to Whitman, there was no other way.

Even so, the possibility seemed remote. After Wilde's death Lord Alfred had been extremely outspoken in print in his defense of Wilde—and then suddenly changed. He had married in 1902 and become a Roman Catholic in 1911, and thus put behind him all such childish things as fellatio, mutual masturbation, sodomy, and so on.

After returning to London from Cambridge I established myself in a small hotel in Suffolk Place called Garland's (which seemed a curious omen to me after the Hamlin Garland experience), and from there telephoned Lord Alfred in Hove.

His voice was high-pitched and tinny over the phone. He seemed cordial enough, and invited me down to tea on an

afternoon two days hence. I found my way to the great blackened ugly skeleton of Victoria Station and took the train to
Brighton in Sussex, which was next door to Hove where he
lived, connected in those days (and perhaps still) by a kind of
boardwalk along the seafront.

My nervousness increased on the way down. He was a lord
of the realm, descended from the Marquess of Queensberry.
I must remember not to mention the names of Robert Ross,
Frank Harris, André Gide—and a host of others who had
been involved in controversy with him—nor even that of
Winston Churchill who had sued Lord Alfred for libel and
won, with Lord Alfred spending six months in the prison of
Wormwood Scrubs as a penalty, all this while he had been
editor of *Plain Speech*. And I must not talk about the Jews or
mention Gertrude Stein, for he was often very obviously
anti-Semitic, even in print. He was the originator of the
quatrain:

How odd
Of God
To choose
The Jews

What, in heaven's name, could we talk about at all?
I found out when we met. The only safe topic was Lord
Alfred Douglas himself.

His address gave me no trouble—St. Ann's Court, Nizell's
Avenue. The stationmaster said that it was not far, a fifteen
minute walk from Brighton past the flimsy pavilions dingy
from the sea air. I turned a corner and found myself facing a
block of flats, perhaps in Regency architecture, little plots
and gates and short sidewalk entrances. It was hardly
Coleridge's countryside "enfolding sunny spots of greenery," nor Wordsworth's "pastoral farms green to the very
door," but it was pleasant and British and the sort of dwell-
ing I was used to seeing in British movies.

He opened the door himself—a man of medium height
with hairline receding on the right side where it was parted,
and the somewhat lackluster straight mousy hair falling
down towards his left eyebrow. His nose was very large and

47

bulbous. The red rose-leaf lips beloved by Wilde had long since vanished; the mouth was compressed and thin, pursed somewhat, and the corners turned slightly downwards. I looked in vain for a hint, even the barest suggestion, of the fair and dreamy youth of the early photographs with Wilde. None was visible. The skin of his face had not suffered the dreadful slackening of the flesh that goes with age; it seemed rather to be of the type that grows old by stretching more tautly over the bones, until—at the end—a skull-like face results. Yet the skin was not stretched tightly enough to pull out the fine network of tiny wrinkles that entirely covered his face and neck.

"Do come in," he said, but then instead of standing aside to let me precede him, he turned and walked ahead of me into the flat, leaving me to shut the door. He looked at me closely and then waved to a chair. "Do sit down," he said.

It was a pleasant room with three or four chairs, rather grimy white curtains at the windows, and a general air of crowding everywhere.

I had been in England just long enough to perceive that most British conversation was all form and no content, a kind of boneless thing, a sort of ping-pong game played without balls. There were no awkward gaps; it ran on and on, pegged to the flimsiest topics—the scenery, the weather of today and yesterday and tomorrow.

Perhaps to put me at ease but more likely to sound me out, Lord Alfred launched into that kind of talk, with a literary flavor. Hemingway was a prurient cad, and Dos Passos a proletarian, probably a Communist (like all left-wingers). Americans do not get enough exercise, and skyscrapers are too too utterly dreadful. Marriage is a mockery in America. If there is another war, the only decent thing for America to do will be to come to Britain's aid immediately; we waited too long in the war of 1914-18—and of course, as Rudyard Kipling pointed out (had I read his poem about that, "The Vineyard," the one that began "At the eleventh hour they came"?), America then took all the credit for winning.

On and on . . . I received a detailed account of the ten or

eleven lawsuits he had been involved in, the trouble he had had over the money of his inheritance, his youthful passions for horse-racing and gambling, his poetry (how much of it had I read, rilly?)—thank you for saying it, yes, he *was* probably England's greatest living poet. Masefield was a poetaster, a hack who had sold his birthright, who had never written a good line after 1930 when he was made Poet Laureate; George Russell ("A.E.") wrote mystical trash . . . And of course Yeats and the other Irish ones—well, you couldn't really call them British poets, now could you?

The pale blue eyes were never still, nor were his hands, nor his feet—for he was continually crossing and recrossing his ankles or tapping his shoe against a nearby chair-leg.

"I suppose," he said suddenly, "you want to hear all about Oscar Wilde and myself!"

By then I think I had analyzed him enough to know that I must disclaim all interest. "Not necessarily," I said with a rather wan smile. "I've read everything that you have written on the subject, and the work of several others . . ."

"Including, I suppose," he said in a fierce voice, "the vile canards and lies of persons like Robbie Ross and Frank Harris and that unspeakable sod André Gide."

"Well, yes . . ." I said lamely.

"Lies, all lies," he said hoarsely, and rose to pace around the room. Had he lived later, doctors would have called him hyperkinetic. He gestured towards the untidy desk. "I am doing a final book on it," he said. "I think I will call it 'Without Apology'."

Suddenly he sat down again, the storm having passed. "Shall we have a spot of tea?" he asked.

"That would be nice."

I took milk in my tea, largely because it was there and it helped to disguise the taste of the brew, which I hated. With the tea he served a small plateful of pink cakes, disastrously sweet, with small silver pellets sprinkled on top, possibly silver-plated buckshot to judge from the internal content.

He never stopped talking—a long monologue in which "As a poet I" and "As an artist I" recurred again and again. He seemed not ever to realize the extent to which he revealed his violent prejudices and hates, nor the immaturity of his view of himself. It became obvious before very long that he had never really grown up. He remained psychologically (and in his own eyes perhaps physically) still the radiant and brilliant adolescent beloved by the gods. He was a man of vast essential egotism yet burdened with a well-concealed inferiority, aggressively insistent on his social position, glossing over his repeated failures in business, and furious with Lord Beaverbrook ("essentially a commoner, donchaknow") for turning down the publication of his poems in the *Evening Standard*, grudge-holding for real and fancied slights, damning White's Club for closing its doors to him . . .

As for homosexual leanings and entanglements—that had all been given up when he became a Catholic—oh yes. He still got hundreds of letters from curiosity seekers and homosexuals and he could have his pick of any of them (my ears and armpits flamed), but that was all finished. Sins of the flesh were obnoxious and uninteresting. I did not know at the time of his liaison with "D.E."—a young person with whom he was infatuated after his wife left him—and all this after he had become a Catholic! These initials were those used by André Gide in telling me, later that summer in Paris, that Lord Alfred had become enamored of "une personne" (feminine gender, but referring in French to either a male or a female) and had been to bed with him/her. There were actually two recorded liaisons: the first with an American girl in 1913 who with jewels and money offered to help Lord Alfred in one of his many litigations, and with whom in his *Autobiography* he admits to "a loss of innocence." The second was a male, a young man sent down from Oxford for low grades, who always introduced himself as the reincarnation of Dorian Gray; and whose camping and good looks and "butterfly devotion" delighted Lord Alfred for over a year in 1925. It was to this young man that Lord Alfred addressed a poem: "To ——— With an Ivory Hand Mirror."

The more he talked, the more I saw the possibility of linking-in with Oscar Wilde fading, along with the afternoon sun. Yet I did not give up. It was inconceivable to me that any man who had spent approximately the first forty years of his life in homosexual activity could have lost those leanings completely on joining the Catholic church. I knew from my own experience. It still seemed to me, as we said in the midwest: "Once one, always one."

And then, since this was still in my drinking days, a happy thought:

In vino veritas.

"Perhaps you will accompany me," I said, "to a nearby pub so that I may buy a round of drinks for us."

He waved his hand. "Hardly necessary, m'boy," he said. "All we need is here. Scotch? Gin and bitters? Sherry?"

"Gin and bitters, please," I had learned to drink it without ice.

And that did it. Within an hour and a half we were in bed, the Church renounced, conscience vanquished, inhibitions overcome, revulsion conquered, pledges and vows and British laws all forgotten. Head down, my lips where Oscar's had been, I knew that I had won.

After I finished my ministrations and settled back, his hand stole down to clamp itself around me. It began to move gently. Still moving it up and down, shafering me, he spoke: "You really needn't have gone to all that trouble, since this is almost all Oscar and I ever did with each other."

Genuinely astonished, I stammered: "B-b-but . . . the poems, and all . . ."

"We used to get boys for each other," he said. "I could always get the workers he liked, and he could get the intellectual ones I preferred. We kissed a lot, but not much more."

I got to Brighton for the ten o'clock train that night. Lord Alfred never wrote to me again, nor I to him. He died in 1945.

In these days it may be of no great interest to those who have graced and honored my bed since 1937 to know that they are directly linked in with Oscar Wilde. But on the other hand if they have a sense of history, they may welcome the information.

From London during that magic summer of 1937 it was on to Paris, and even today, recalling the excitement of that first visit to the heartland of art and literature, the feeling remains hard to define. It was like a slight trembling of the fringe around one's soul, a vague and not unpleasant quivering of the secret marrow deep in the bones, a prickling in the skin that made one restless and yet content.

Come April or October in Paris, it is all the same—the golden hazy afternoons, the life of the cafés, the sweet grey spirit of the old city. And when you breathe and look and listen—no matter whether you have seen one or a score of springs or summers in Paris, you know that this is the very best season Paris ever had.

Paris had always been the holy city of artists, writers, and composers, and in the year I arrived the subtle ghosts of the great were still strolling the boulevards and drinking in the cafés. The treasures of the Louvre acted like a magnet on my art hungry soul, and in the Golden Age of Paris no other city could compare with it. For me she was the City of Light, looking like a queen in a book, with a wreath of pearls in her raven hair and a bright brooch at her breast—at her best she was like that, and all men and some women must adore. She was the grave yet smiling, serenely great Grey Lady of the cities of the world.

I was young and romantic and laid open to all the city's charms. When I had tasted as many of them as I could, I remembered that André Gide had also invited me to come to see him whenever I arrived in Paris.

His name is nearly forgotten today for some reason—but he was one of the first writers of the twentieth century who dared openly to confess his homosexuality in print. He produced two classics of homosexual literature: *The Counterfeiters* and *The Immoralist,* as well as a very early Platonic dialogue on the subject—*Corydon*—in 1911. Unabashed, he could write—and be accepted for writing—a haunting sentence about the Arab boys whom he loved: "More precisely, I was attracted to them by what remained of the sun on their brown skins"; and could in 1920 say in print: "In the name of what God or what ideal do you forbid me to live according to my nature? . . . My normal is your abnormal, and your normal is my abnormal." These were strong statements indeed for those early years, especially when it is remembered that despite France's reputation for tolerance, the basic tradition in that country was heterosexual, that of a man for his wife and mistress. Homosexuality, when it occasionally reached the public press, was referred to as an "outrage of manners/taste" (*outrage des moeurs*), later modified to "une affaire rose."

In my callow literary judgment of the time Gide did not measure up to such other "greats" as Thomas Mann and Romain Rolland, but he was nonetheless important to me, because his brave and brilliant stand for homosexuality was like a lighthouse in those dark and stormy days of the 1930s. His writing lacked the realism of today, of course, but it had skill, comprehension, and talent, and understanding of the human heart. To many, Gide's writing was thin, but to me in my twenties he was one of the first knights of Camelot.

It is difficult to say what was in my mind that muggy Parisian afternoon in August when I sought out his address on the rue Vaneau, climbed a flight of stairs, and very timidly rapped at the door. I was quite nervous and a little frightened.

Neither Gide nor a maid answered my knock. Instead it was an eighteen-year-old Arab boy. He was like a very handsome young Roman, dark and bronzelike with splendidly chiseled nose and mouth, and (to borrow a phrase from a letter of Wilde's) the tents of midnight were folded in his eyes; moons hid in their curtains. His face rose like a classic sculpture above the straight lines of his white burnoose, and on his head was a tasseled red *chéchia*, a fez.

"I am expected by Monsieur Gide," I gulped in French.

"De la part de qui?" His teeth gleamed in a curve of white. "Who is it?"

I was so overwhelmed by his beauty that all French momentarily deserted me, but it soon came back. I gave him my name and he asked me to wait in the study. I sat down, dumbstruck by his beauty, and he disappeared.

It was a very untidy room with piles of books here and there—stacked on the floor and filling many shelves. A decrepit old typewriter stood on the scarred desk, and the windows were closed with louvered shutters. A moment's panic rose in me, for what reason I did not know, a feeling, a subcurrent of something almost evil and mysterious. Perhaps it was the heat, or the claustrophobic sensation induced by the shuttered room.

And then André Gide entered. He was a tall, slightly stooped man in his late sixties, wearing a shabby old unbuttoned brown cardigan sweater that sagged from somewhat narrow shoulders. His shirt had no collar, but was secured at the neck below his mobile Adam's apple by a brass collar stud. The face was sensitive and thin-lipped, and he was nearly bald save at the back of his head. His cheekbones were high and hollowed underneath—the sort of face in which Lombroso would have seen Gide's troublesome puritan-Protestantism reflected.

"Monsieur," he said, shaking hands with the usual short sharp French snap. "I am enchanted to meet you." And then he looked around the room. "This is not an inviting place to talk. Let us go to another room which may be more comfortable."

It was one of those characteristic long French "railroad" apartments, with rooms opening on each side of a central corridor. In one of them with an open door sat the young Arab who had let me in, nearly naked and cross-legged on a bed, sewing a fine seam in his burnoose which he had removed and laid across one knee.

"What an extraordinarily handsome young man," I murmured to Gide.

"Yes," he said in English. "He is one of the most beautiful creatures I have ever seen." He smiled. "I speak a little the English. If he hears a compliment one cannot live with him . . . the rest of the day." Then he switched to French again. "In here," he said, opening another door at the end of the hall.

It was an amazing room. It had a huge circular bed draped with a pink satin coverlet, and a frilly canopy at one end. Circular beds were very rare indeed in 1937.

Gide sat down in a noisy wicker chair with his back towards the windows. "I hope the monsieur will excuse me," he said. "The light is very painful to my eyes."

He had the habit of a small cough which constantly interrupted his speech—not exactly asthmatic, but dry and a little rasping. "It is a great pleasure to meet Americans. My books seem to be more popular in your country than in mine. And I thank you for your letters. They have been most moving . . . most flattering."

"Thank you very much," I said. "Yes, your work is very popular in the States," adding that in a course in the modern novel I included his *The Counterfeiters* and much admired its experimental structure.

He smiled. "I wanted to call the translation *The Coiners*, but Madame Knopf said that such a term would not be as well understood."

"We have just finished reading your *Return from the USSR*," I said.

"And that too," he said. "I thought 'Back from' would be more forceful than 'Return' but once again Madame Knopf said no. Women are strong in America. One wonders whether she or her husband is the publisher."

"You were gravely disappointed with Russia," I said.

"Ah!" he said, striking his forehead with the palm of his hand. "That is hardly the word. I was profoundly disillusioned. So much there, so wonderful, so fascinating. I went there expecting to find the new race, the handsome young men, the workers . . . and all I found was a state headed for the worst kind of dictatorship of the few, those high in the party. And no freedom at all in sexual matters, except marriage and divorce. It has gone the way of all great centralized powers." He smiled again. "I apologize, but your country must be included. Have you been to the Exposition yet?"

I nodded.

"Then you have seen the two pavilions—the Russian with the hammer and sickle on its facade, confronting the German eagle and the swastika directly across the way. I find that extremely symbolic. And it will be all too short a time, I fear, until Germany and Russia really do confront each other. It will be Armageddon; we will all be destroyed."

I thought that perhaps it would be wise to try to turn him to another topic. "What do you think of American writers?"

"I like many of them," he said. "There is Steinbeck— such simplicity and understanding. And empathy with his characters. His *Cannery Row* is beautiful."

"And *The Grapes of Wrath*?"

"I did not like that too much. It was very painful."

"*The Immoralist* was a painful book too," I said, "at least for some of us. You had the courage to speak out about 'the problem' here in France when few others dared touch the subject. What do you think of Hemingway?" I went on, like a reporter.

The Gallic hand vibrated in front of his face. "No, no," he said forcefully. "He is too . . . too physical. One can see through the hairy chest. He is a poseur. He pretends to be a man but all the time struggles against what he really is— else why the overwhelming male friendships in all his works?"

I wanted to get the word out of him. "Do you mean you think him homosexual?"

Gide smiled and shrugged. "It is not for me to say."

"What other writers do you like?"

"Faulkner. He did a splendid piece of work in *Sanctuary*, but nothing since. And Dos Passos is interesting. Some critics claim he is a disciple of mine. And Michael Gold— such feeling, such pity for the Jews."

"Gold has been bitter against homosexuals," I said, thinking of Wilder. "Do you like Dreiser?"

"I can't read him. He is too . . . lumpy. Too ungrammatical."

I smiled to hear the current titan of American letters so easily cast aside. "A lot of critics feel that the floral period of the American novel was the 1920s," I said. "Wharton, Wilder, Hemingway, Willa Cather . . ."

"Who is Cather? I have not heard of him."

I explained gently that she was a woman, and then asked, "Have you ever thought of coming to America?"

"I am afraid of New York," he said.

"A lot of persons are," I said. "But they would be very kind to you."

"Ah, yes . . . perhaps *too* kind. I would like to go incognito but that is not possible. Even in Russia I was recognized. I do not think I would be physically able to stand your great country."

Shifting topics a bit, I told him that I had seen Lord Alfred Douglas in England. His eyebrows went up.

"A dreadful man," he said. "A shocking man."

"Will you ever write any more about Wilde and Lord Alfred?" I asked.

"I think not," he said. "There is my little book on Oscar Wilde that pleased Robert Ross so much, and the passages in *Si le Grain ne Meurt*. I have said most of what I wanted to say."

It was a short interview but I did not want to tire him. "Your *chef d'oeuvre*," I said, holding out a copy of the French edition of *The Counterfeiters*. "Would you be kind enough to sign it for me?"

"Delighted," he said. "It is always flattering." He took the book and inscribed an elegantly phrased sentiment, pausing to make sure of the exact spelling of my name. At the door he said "Au revoir" and then delivered himself of a short speech deploring the lack of an exact American equivalent for the expression. "I hope that you will come to see me again when I am recovered from my recent travels."

I assured him that I would. He took down my address at the Hôtel Récamier and promised to give me a *coup de téléphone* soon.

I thanked him, not expecting to hear from him again. But about ten days later the patronne at the hotel, much impressed, told me that Monsieur Gide had phoned and left a message which said: "Can you come this evening at nine o'clock?"

Of course. Gide himself met me at the door. "I have a little surprise for you," he said, handing me an inscribed copy of his novel, *Les Caves du Vatican.*

"I am overwhelmed." I said.

"Ah, but that is not really the surprise," he said. "Come with me."

Once again we went down the long corridor towards the room with the circular bed. He half-opened the door and I went in, and then to my amazement he closed the door again with himself on the outside.

Lighted only by the frilly little pink tulip-lamp on the bed table, the young Arab who had opened the door for me on my first visit sensually stretched his naked limbs on the bed and smiled, and held out his arms in invitation.

"I am Ali," he said.

Small wonder that I have never forgotten the works of Gide.

GERTRUDE AND ALICE

Two weeks of that magic summer of 1937 were spent at Bilignin in southern France as the guest of Gertrude Stein and Alice B. Toklas, two weeks of a golden romp with them, afternoons of excursions to dream over the lovely French countryside, evenings of delicious meals prepared by Alice, and days of feeling that life was wonderful and exciting, with such a flood of happy recollections rushing to the screen of memory in recalling those days at Bilignin that it is hard to enfold them in a capsule of time and space, especially since the two weeks were repeated two years later, and the two visits happily mingled in mind and memory.

At the moment of happening in 1937, however, a highly nervous youngish man of twenty-eight—suffering from a Pernod hangover that should have ended forever all the love I had for alcohol—descended from the train at Culoz and looked around an empty station. Anise was reeking from every pore; I walked enveloped in a cloud of scent from the wicked greenish liqueur. The train had gone puffing on towards Marseille—and the globe of silence it had left behind was profound, so deep that within it I heard the small singing of the blood in my ears.

There was no sign of Gertrude and Alice. I heard, then, some locusts somewhere, and the faroff tinkle of a cowbell. A cart moved nearby over cobblestones. Within the station one could almost hear the paint peeling from the walls, a faded brown and beige. There was a sudden crash, as of a box being dropped, and I went inside in search of the noise.

A station attendant—blue coveralls, a sweat-stained red handkerchief knotted at his neck, complete with dusty beret and walrus mustache—was upending another box from a baggage cart. In my then halting French I asked him if he knew the two American ladies from Belley or Bilignin.

"Ah," he said, "but certainly, monsieur."

"Have you seen them today?"

In a torrent of rapid French I heard that they often came to shop in Culoz, but that he had not seen them for more than two weeks, and certainly not on this day, but perhaps monsieur would like to telephone them at Bilignin. He collected some francs from me and showed me the station telephone.

I was dismayed but brave. French telephones frightened me. I had to make the operator understand what I wanted, spelling out Stein, and when I finally reached the house at Bilignin it was to speak with Madame Roux, the housekeeper, and she spoke a patois beyond me.

I did manage to understand that they were not there, that they had gone to Culoz to meet *"un jeune américain."* Yes, I said, I was the one. I hung up, checked my suitcase, and set out to try to find them.

An hour of walking passed. I could not know that as I was going down one narrow street, they were going up another. They had decided to do some shopping before the train arrived, and had consequently not been at the station when it did. Gradually many of the townspeople of Culoz were out looking for us, trying to bring us together, for half the village had seen one or the other of us wandering around. At that time I had not yet heard Gertrude say: "I hate meeting trains and saying goodbye to them and meeting people and seeing them go away" or I would have been even more upset than I was.

59

At last I returned to the station and unchecked my baggage, and sat down on it to wait—a thing I should have done in the first place. Within five minutes, Gertrude and Alice appeared at the top of a street leading down.

"Jesus," I said to myself, starting towards them.

"Damnation!" Gertrude shouted. "There he is, the lost is found, it's Sammy himself!"

We spent the next half hour alternately swearing and explaining, while they looked at me and I looked at them.

Gertrude was in a pink silk brocaded vest with a pale yellow crêpe de Chine blouse. Her skirt was monk's-cloth, a sort of homespun burlap, and she wore flat-heeled shoes. Alice's hat was wild with fruits and flowers, yellow and red; her dress was black, and triple loops of purple beads swung down to her waist. I forced myself not to stare at her faint mustache nor even at Gertrude's short-cut grey hair circling in a fascinating whorl at the back of her head. Her craggy face was like the profile on a Roman coin.

We climbed into the Matford and set off, with Gertrude driving and Alice sitting sidewise on the back seat, filing her nails.

The first evening was memorable. They lived in a seventeenth-century chateau which they rented every summer, with a mansard roof and a small formal garden behind it. "Tumbledown," Gertrude called it, but to me it seemed charming and in good repair. It was lovely and old, with gleaming hardwood floors, and a stone stairway to the second floor. The garden had plots of trimmed box hedges with dark lustrous leaves, and Gertrude pointed out to me the broad beautiful valley sloping casually down to the Ain River and rising again to a circle of misty blue unforgettable hills, with the barely visible peak of Mont Blanc far in the distance, rosy and golden in the setting sun.

Then Gertrude showed me my room, and the bathroom—of which she was very proud. She turned on the hot water in the washbowl and it came out with a great gush of steam. "There, what do you think of that," she said. "We just had it put in. All that water as soon as a hotel and hotter too."

Evenings, we sat in the drawing room, happy after the

wonderful meals that Alice prepared. In the blue paper-thin china cups the after-dinner infusions of verveine cooled. There was a great squeaking rocking chair which was Gertrude's alone, and its gentle noise, the happy squeaking song, remains the all-pervasive sound of Bilignin that has fastened itself in memory. By the tempo of its sound, sometimes slow as old Time, and sometimes under the pressure of Gertrude's excitement rapid and allegro, punctuating her sentences like the commas she disdained, you could judge just how well or how poorly the evening's talk was going. It was Gertrude's chair, and Alice never sat in it, nor any guest. She rocked against the background of white woodwork and painted trompe l'oeil panels of corbeils and hunting horns, and musical instruments in tones of grey, brown, soft yellow, and faded purple. The smoke of cigarettes drifted lazily out into the burst of rose and gold that fell upon the garden. And we talked of everything under the sun—of the ballet, of Wally Simpson and her duke, of gardens, scenery, Mussolini, politics, teaching, salads and herbs and dressings, gasoline and spiders and cuckoos. The timbre of Gertrude's voice was rich and deep, and her great laugh—booming out over the valley—was the throat-filling laughter of the Valkyries.

Mornings, Gertrude did not come down until late, and we generally took a walk before lunch, as well as another before dinner—either the "upper turn" through green and brown vineyards with the grapes fragrant upon the vines, or the "lower turn" down towards the river, among the cool of the trees, walking on a cushion of leaves and moss and loam. And always the talk—of how the mutter of threatening summer storms made the farmers fear for their grapes, of the painting of Sir Francis Rose, of literature and her theories, of dipsomania and the authors who fell into it, of Roman roads in France.

In the afternoons there were usually automobile trips here and there. Gertrude and Alice delighted in showing the quiet French countryside to their friends. Sometimes it was a flying trip to the Chambéry markets for meat and vegetables, or to Belley for rice and olive oil. Sometimes it was a party for the colony of *surréalistes* under André Breton, meeting Matta and Yves Tanguy, or a trip to the Abbey of Hautecombe for an hour with their Benedictine friends. Once we went on a journey to Geneva to see the Spanish paintings from the Prado that had been sent to Switzerland for safekeeping during the Spanish Civil War, with a pause for luncheon in a field, eating a delicious chicken that Alice had steamed over white wine and herbs. Again it was a lively discussion with Henry and Clare Booth Luce at Aix-les-Bains about a proposed collaboration on a play. Now it was a trip to Virieu-le-Grand and a small agricultural fair, with butter in molds shaped like small sheep, nine-inch mushrooms, and Gertrude firing at the whirling tin grouse in a shooting gallery. Or it was a ride in the cool dusk, the fragrant twilight, to Artemare, to eat *terrine* of duck, tomatoes in oil, partridge and thin crusted potatoes, with tiny wild strawberries which Madame Berrard's son had picked in the hills that afternoon.

I was not old enough then—nor indeed was anyone wise enough at that time—to evaluate accurately her place in literature; and certainly it was hard to be conscious of it while one was near her. Often I was overwhelmed by her presence—while we were walking, or talking—and by the fact that I had been permitted the rare privilege and pleasure of visiting her. I remember her as a great and very human woman, an intricate yet simple and earthy personality, tremendously alive. I think of her on a rainy day in a small garage, down on hands and knees on the oily floor discussing the axle of her car with a young mechanic. I remember how we worked together in her garden, both bent over hoes as we weeded the tomatoes. I see her walking along the dusty roadways, switching her dogleash at the ragweed as she talked, and now and then shouting to Pepe, the little Mexican chihuahua that Picabia had given her, to stop chasing chickens. I see her turn quickly away from the sight of a helpless calf with its legs tied for market, saying "Let us not look at that." I hear her hearty laugh as she showed me how, with one quick movement, she had mastered the French peasant's trick of catching a napkin under both arms at once.

On one odd afternoon when only Gertrude and I were in the car, the mood slowly changed and became strangely intimate. Alice had been left behind by her own choice, while Gertrude and I were sent on an errand to Belley for milk and oil. We had been talking of my projected trip to Algiers, the dangers of being alone in the Casbah—and then the topics had shifted, so that she was asking me questions about my parents and about the two maiden aunts who had brought me up.

Suddenly, while still driving, she grabbed my kneecap and squeezed it hard. "Sammy," she said, "do you think Alice and I are lesbians?"

I was startled. A curl of flame ran up my spine. "It's no one's business one way or another," I said.

"Do you care whether we are," she asked.

"Not in the least," I said, suddenly dripping wet.

"Are *you* queer or gay or different or 'of it' as the French say or whatever they are calling it nowadays," she said, still driving as fast as always. She had let go my knee.

I waggled my hand. "I'm currently both," I said. "I think," I added. "I don't see why I should go limping on one leg through life just to satisfy a so-called norm."

There was not very much more to the conversation. She said that she and Alice had always been surrounded by homosexuals, that they both liked all people who produced—"and what they do in bed is their own business, and what we do is not theirs." She had denigrated male homosexuals to Hemingway to see if he would squirm because he was a secret one. And then after those shattering few moments that day she never referred to the matter again. She and Alice were very private persons, really Victorian—completely monogamous, abstemious, and on the surface more than a little reserved.

On another extraordinary afternoon Gertrude sat in her rocking chair, her feet on the cross-bar between the two rocker-ends while she read aloud to me her recently completed book for children, *The World Is Round*. Her voice was mellow, and pitched somewhere between alto and

63

baritone—yet it could rise higher if the reading demanded it, and then it would take on a husky almost whispery quality. But usually it lived in the lower range—deeply resonant as if there were an extra secret chamber within her which gave depth and body to her tones. And when that wonderful instrument exploded in laughter, as it so frequently did, there was an infectious quality to it which compelled everyone to join in—a deep booming laughter that carried over the whole of their small domain and spilled down the garden wall into the valley. So she read to me in that voice, its cadences timed by the counterpoint of the wicker chair rocking, weaving its high reedy voice around hers, filling the interstices and underlining the human quality of her tones. There was no way at that early time to capture the golden rotundities of her voice, save to carve it deeply into my conscious memory, for tape recorders then—using wire—were as cumbersome and unwieldy as a suitcase.

It was not possible for the visits to Gertrude and Alice to be oil-smooth all of the time. It seemed to me that I was responsible for an unconscionable number of gaffes. One of the mildest occurred when the three of us were riding to Chambéry one afternoon to do some shopping. I wanted a cigarette, and since I was in the front seat I pushed in the electric lighter on the dashboard. Then with my mind on something Gertrude was saying, I very casually tossed the lighter out the open window.

It had no sooner left my hand than I howled with the realization. Gertrude's foot went down heavily on the brake, and Alice was dislodged from her Madame Récamier position in the back seat.

"What's the matter, my god, what's the matter, Sammy," Gertrude asked.

I told them what I had done. Gertrude laughed and backed up a hundred yards. "Calm down," she said to me, for I was trembling. "We'll find it."

And she did, spotting it almost at once by the roadside.

I was still shaken. In Chambéry Alice, to quiet me, bought me a serrated tomato-slicing knife, a beautiful small thing exactly like the one she had at Bilignin. And that night I slipped downstairs to her sacred kitchen, found her knife in the drawer, and substituted the new one for her old one . . . a more personal remembrance than the shiny new blade. I often wondered if her sharp eye caught the difference, and presumed that it had.

On another occasion while I was in the garden reading one of the manuscript volumes of *Everybody's Autobiography* which Gertrude was in the process of writing, Alice called to me to go with them, again to shop. I put the volume upside down on the low garden wall, where it remained overnight. The next morning I was scolded by Alice—but soon forgiven when she saw how intense my chagrin was.

"There, there—no harm done," she said, "and I won't tell Gertrude. But it was lucky, really. Suppose it had rained—where would the manuscript be?"

But by far the most awful of the episodes happened as I was packing my things to leave on a trip to Algiers. Gertrude and Alice had retired and shut their bedroom door, which angled with the bathroom door. I was in the bathroom, stuffing my toiletries into their case. The light was on and I had left the door open. I was being as quiet as I could, thinking they might already be asleep.

Suddenly I heard their bedroom door open and looked up, startled. There at the bathroom entrance stood Gertrude, completely naked. She covered her pubis quickly with both hands, said "Whoops!" in a loud voice, and vanished back into her bedroom, slamming the door so hard the bathroom mirror rattled. I had only the barest quickest glimpse of her, but my shocked eyes noted the glistening hollow pink scar that remained from the excision of part of her left breast. As I stuttered something like "I was just packing—" she was at the same time saying "I thought you'd left the light on in the bathroom—"

Upset and trembling, I made it back to my room—for aside from the doctors who had delivered her and operated on her (if they were men) I was convinced that I was the only male who had ever seen her naked. With shaking hands I poured myself a large drink of my "emergency" cognac and went to sleep with nightmares. But the next morning, bland as Buddha, Gertrude said nothing about it at all.

When I returned from three weeks of adventuring in Algiers, war was in the air. Sir Francis Rose and Cecil Beaton had my former room, so I slept in another. Everyone was tense and frightened, and we all hovered around a small radio Francis had. Tiring finally of the same bulletins endlessly repeated, I wandered out into the rose garden. Cecil Beaton was there reclining in a canvas chair. He wore a thin jacket over a light summer sweater with broad red and white horizontal stripes, and one of Gertrude's high-crowned Korean straw hats. He had on a pair of khaki walking shorts and was fiddling with a rose in one hand while he seemed to be sketching the Ain Valley with the other.

"Why aren't you listening to the war broadcasts?" I asked.

"Ch—chamberlain ... has ar ... arranged things," he said. " 'll be no war." His slurred speech indicated he was completely drunk.

I beckoned Francis out of the living room. "You know Gertrude's rules about alcohol," I said. "Cecil is smashed."

The remark galvanized Francis. "My God," he said. We went out towards the chair. It was empty, save for the sketch pad and straw hat. Cecil had vanished.

So began a wild afternoon. Francis and I went looking for him on the road to Belley, but he was nowhere to be found. Meanwhile the sky had clouded over, and later in the after-noon a drizzle began. It grew darker.

"You'll have to tell Gertrude," I said.

"You do it," Francis said. "I'm really afraid to."

"Not I," I said. "You march right in and tell her."

He did. There was a loud bellow from the house, and soon Gertrude came out wearing a kind of droopy Garbo raincoat. Francis was behind her.

The next few hours were a mad mixture of phone calls, instructions from Gertrude to tell the mayor, to call out the troops from the caserne. ("With all due respect to Made-moiselle Stein," shrugged one gendarme, "war is near, and after all it is only one man. He will be found when dawn comes.")

At one point I was left in Belley to check the bistros. Cecil was in none of them. I consoled myself with a drink at a café. And finally the auto came around the corner from Bilignin, Gertrude at the wheel, Alice and Francis in back and between them a very wet and bedraggled Cecil.

"Where on earth—?" I asked.

They told me that Cecil had been at the caserne all afternoon, drinking and learning Senegalese songs from the huge black Senegalese quartered in the barracks there ("and heaven knows what else was going on," said Francis sotto voce to me), and that two six-feet-four Senegalese soldiers had been walking him home, all fairly snockered, and singing "L'Alouette" at the top of their lungs.

Francis said, "I told him to behave while he was here, but you know Cecil. Show him a ..." He broke off and looked straight ahead.

"Well, all is quiet now," I said. "The lost sheep is found."

Cecil struggled upwards from his collapsed position but Alice pushed him back down. " ... no sheep," he muttered.

That night—although we did not need it—Gertrude warned us all to leave before the military commandeered all the trains, and we departed the next morning, finding our way home as best we could. Gertrude and Alice stayed behind. When I got back to America after strenuous vexations I sent them a Mixmaster—which delighted them both, and was the subject of several playful letters from Gertrude.

I did not see her again. On July 27, 1946, the newspapers carried the word to the world of her death. On that evening there were many empty hearts in the world, and many lonely people remembered her. I walked long along the lake front in Chicago, almost as sadly lost as the young Tennyson who—hearing of the death of Byron—crawled out upon a finger of land jutting into the sea, and carved upon a rock the words: "Byron is dead." With him an age came to an end, and so, too, was a door closed with the death of Gertrude Stein.

It was not possible for me to get to Paris again until 1950 to see Alice. But the letters from her began at once after Gertrude died, and her strong and vital personality emerged from the shadow in which she had deliberately kept it during Gertrude's lifetime. They were often voluminous, done with the thinnest nib in the delicate spiderwork that was her handwriting, which Mercedes de Acosta said was done with the "eyelash of a fly." She wrote on both sides of translucent paper, so that one side confused the other. The letters were filled with humor and tidbits of gossip, sharp and often hilarious, witty and sometimes sentimental. Many years later, in 1977, over a hundred letters to me from Gertrude and Alice—together with a lengthy memoir of them—were published by Houghton Mifflin under the title *Dear Sammy*.

Alice had gone on living at 5 rue Christine, where all the paintings were. The maid ushered me into the salon—with its walls covered with the work of Picasso, Matisse, Juan Gris, Picabia, and others. I sat down on the shabby old horsehair sofa on which Gertrude used to curl up, directing the chatter of the salon, talking in that warm golden voice which would not ever again call me her "silly, bashful boy."

There were red roses in a white china vase on the table; I laid my bouquet beside them. It was quiet; the clatter of Paris was stilled. A huge ornamented silver tray with tea things was on the table in front of the sofa. Through the ceiling-high French windows I looked out upon the chimney pots in the quiet enclosure formed by the tight-pressed houses—and the flat roof on which the aging deaf and blind old Basket went to do his little duties, and from which he had fallen fifteen feet at midnight.

And Alice? She was the same—a little more bent, more drawn, frail, tiny, and wispy. Somehow, however, the essence had not changed. She had gone on being fond of me through all the time that we had been apart.

The years from then until her death in 1967 were full of the business of living for both of us. I had taken a small vacation from teaching to do a major rewriting and editorial job for an encyclopedia, and then gone back to teaching in a different university, even worse than the preceding one, and had finally renounced Akademia to shock my colleagues by becoming a tattoo artist. And every Christmas from 1952 until her death I visited Alice in Paris.

They were years of both happiness and pain for us. I watched her grow older and poorer, as she also watched me age. She supported me when I finally abandoned the grape entirely; and I was amazed when she joined the Catholic Church, brought to it by a priest who assured her that in the afterlife she would see Gertrude again. When we were together at the Christmas season we gossiped like old ladies over a back fence. I was able to tell her all the details ("I eat 'em with a spoon," she used to say cheerfully) about how Sir Francis Rose had unwittingly hired his illegitimate son as his "valet de chambre," and screwed him for four months before learning his true identity. To her question about how I knew all of it I could answer that I was the one who had first pointed out the young man to Francis, and sent him waddling after him. And I met her in Rome for some hilarious adventures among the seven hills. There were painful moments such as the one when—returning from a winter spent in a convent at Rome—she found her apartment stripped bare of all the paintings, confiscated by the greedy widow of Gertrude's nephew on the ground that left alone the paintings were "a national treasure left unprotected." Alice's last years were spent under the financial protection of friends, of whom Donald Sutherland and Thornton Wilder were the leading contributors, the others of the group giving only dribbles.

The most emotional moment with her occurred one day in Paris while we were lunching at La Méditerranée, a restaurant frequented in the old days by Gertrude and Alice and many of their friends—Pablo, Bébé, Gerald, Cecil, and Francis. We sat with our jugged hare at a table near some workmen who were enlarging the restaurant with an additional room. Just as we started to eat, the foreman of the workers approached Alice with beret in hand, and started to speak in French.

"Mademoiselle," he was saying, and with that she extended her left hand for him to kiss lightly, "Mademoiselle, I am only a humble worker but I have seen you here many times and at the opera and elsewhere, and I hope that you will permit me to thank you for bringing to our city the luster that you and Mademoiselle Stein have brought for so many years. And we thank you for living among us." He bowed his head over her hand again and was gone.

"Wh-what was that?" I stuttered.

"Ah," said Alice, "he was remembering the old days."

Then the full meaning of the gesture hit me, and I reacted with great emotion, blinded by a sudden flood of tears as I realized the historic importance of Gertrude and Alice. I tried to eat and at the same time hide my weeping from her, but could not succeed at either. She closed her hand over mine and said, "Now Sammy, stop it this instant. We who are left behind can only wait." And the wait was long for her—twenty-one years.

Gertrude's tombstone in the cemetery of Père-Lachaise has graven on its reverse side the facts of Alice's life—name, birthplace, and dates. And when she died, they opened Gertrude's grave and placed her smaller coffin beside the larger one. The inscription around the tomb of Héloïse and Abelard—down the hill in the same cemetery—might well have been reworded for this double grave:

> Here at long last the ashes of
> Gertrude and Alice are reunited.

THORNTON AND THE TOUCH OF EROS

At the end of those first two weeks at Bilignin in that magic summer of 1937, it was time to leave, for a lunch had been arranged with Thomas Mann at Kusnacht near Zurich. This had been long planned, but Gertrude was not aware of it. The day before my departure she asked me if I knew Thornton Wilder.

"I met him once eight years ago in 1929," I said, "and asked him to sign *The Angel That Troubled the Waters.*

Gertrude Stein's right hand.

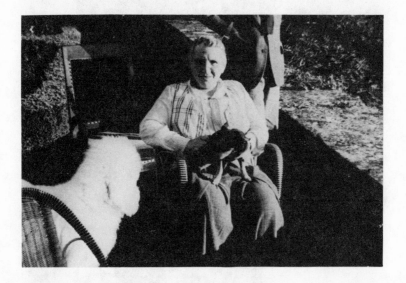

Gertrude Stein with Basket and Pepi in 1937.

Gertrude Stein at a shooting gallery in 1937.

The author with Alice B. Toklas on the terrace at 5 rue Christine, Paris, 1952.

The author as a "sailor" at Brest in 1954.

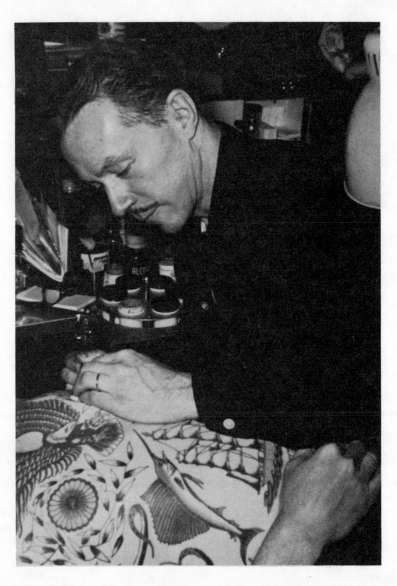

Phil Sparrow at work.

Thornton Wilder in the room where Oscar Wilde died,
Hotel d'Alsace, Paris, 1937.

The author in 1977.

Scott.

But he would not remember me."

"Well," she said, "you're going to Zurich and I am going to write him a note and you can say hello to him. He's writing a play just now and I think it may be a good one."

I was in Zurich from September 11th to the 17th. During that week—or rather, following one memorable night—Thornton wrote the last act of *Our Town*.

My feelings about him in 1937 were different from those of the first time we had met. I was eight years older and considered myself much more knowledgeable—the levels of sophistication change every decade. Another thing marking a shift in my opinions about Thornton was Michael Gold's attack on him in *The New Republic* in 1930. Echoes of that vicious slashing assault had never left my mind, and phrases still hung in the valleys, for Gold had called Wilder a prophet of the genteel Christ, the Emily Post of culture, producer of a chambermaid literature peopled with daydreams of homosexual figures in graceful gowns. Gold was simply following the Communist party line of attack, but I was not astute enough at the time to recognize it.

The criticism had affected me so much that I had almost lost interest in Wilder. I had not read anything of his since our first meeting except *Heaven's My Destination*, which I found totally unlike his previous writing. In fact, I liked it a great deal—a picaresque accounting of the adventures of a "pure fool." But in the ladder of my ranking of literary favorites, Thornton had slipped considerably. Still, Gertrude said "Meet him"—so meet him I did, but without great enthusiasm.

Our week began with a whirlwind of talk—eager, lively, and fascinating to me. The richness of his mind reminded me of that of Oscar Wilde, and I wondered if Thornton—like Wilde—exhausted his resources in talk instead of writing, the urge to put things on paper diminished by the audience for his conversation. He excused himself somewhat by saying that he had spoken nothing but German for so long that he was delighted now to return to English.

Our talk was wide-ranging. And of what? Of Japanese warlords, of Siegfried's lime leaf, the meaning of the Greek

71

word *olisbos,* the death of tattooing, the superiority of drama over the novel, of Druid rites and curses and runes and Stonehenge, and the nature of the Eleusinian mysteries as Sir James Frazer described them. Early on I discovered that he had scores of little set speeches, and these issued forth automatically when properly triggered; such reactions are usual in schoolmasters (of whom I was one) who talk so much they forget what they have said to whom.

During those days in Zurich we saw each other every afternoon and evening; his mornings were devoted to writing, or attempting it, for he confessed that he was blocked at the end of the second act of the play he was composing. As Boswell reported of Goldsmith when he was around Dr. Johnson, Thornton seemed to have a great desire to "shine" for my benefit. Or perhaps it was just that he had not had an American to talk *to*—not *with*—for a number of days.

I recognized that many of his ideas had come from Gertrude Stein—and he was frank to admit it.

"But I really can't understand her writing," he said. "Try as I may, there are clouds and darkness over the land, so much of it."

"But you've done the introductions to *Narration* and *The Geographical History* . . ." I protested.

"Largely based on our conversations together," he said. "Our exchanges of ideas. She is very clear to me when she *speaks* about writing and thinking. And in much of her writing I feel the authority of what she says, even though it may not be at all clear to me."

We had progressed from the bar of the Carleton-Elite, where we had met, to the dining room, still talking furiously, he doing most of it and myself listening. At meal-end we got started on religion, and I found myself denigrating the Catholic church, and telling him of the various sad experiences with western priests in Montana.

Thornton listened for a while and then suddenly slapped his hand down flat on the tablecloth. A large orange, perched precariously on top of a *corbeille* of fruits on our table, rolled off and across the floor. A waiter, scowling, picked it up and restored it to its place. Thornton never paused in his talking.

"Don't say those things!" he exclaimed. "Because, suppose—just *suppose* the Catholic church may be the right answer to all we are looking for!" And then he went on, tracing the line of authority through the New Testament down to the Reformation until I was quite wearied with the bottle I had uncorked. He was religion-haunted all his life, repeatedly asking the unanswerable question and ever waiting for a sign.

Then he returned to talking about Gertrude, full of stories and anecdotes.

"I can praise her to men but not to women," he said, looking intently and somewhat owlishly at me through his glasses. "Women don't want to hear about her. She seems to be the only woman today who is seriously trying to develop a metaphysical mind, and that impulse overwhelms the feminine in her. I myself have never 'come clear' to her, I think. She eyes me constantly—"

"As she did me," I said, fiddling with the brandy glass. "I frequently caught her at it."

"She does that when she doesn't understand a person. She's writing the second volume of her autobiography—"

"Yes, she let me read it," I said, and told him of the horrible mishap when I had left the manuscript on the garden wall all night.

Thornton laughed. "You were lucky to get out of that one," he said. "And singularly honored to be permitted to read it. It's a fascinating volume—it will *go*—but I don't like the 'ballet' ending. Seemed awfully gabby to me. Still, I wouldn't dare criticize anything she did."

"Oh my," I said. "I did, once or twice."

"It's a wonder she didn't throw you out," he chuckled. "As her literary executor I often find myself worried silly about what may happen after she dies. What Alice may say and do. Alice can be difficult."

"Alice may die first," I said.

Of the six or seven afternoons and evenings with Thornton in Zurich, there was one extraordinary night when it started to rain while we were walking around the town—not hard, mostly a drizzle. He had been telling me about the establishment of milkbars in Switzerland to combat the growing incidence of alcoholism among the young (with perhaps a slanting reference to my own drinking in those days), and talking about his visit with Freud, and how Freud had rather obliquely suggested that Thornton and Freud's daughter Anna would make a good match. Then he somehow got started about the historical Zurich, and the writers it had harbored there over the years.

And so in the light rain a kind of lengthy literary pilgrimage began. I kept getting drunker and drunker, hardly able to pass a bar without getting another cognac ("to ward off a cold," I said) while he steered me to the Café Odéon to see the spot where Tristan Tzara read laundry lists into poetry and invented Dada to shock the intellectual complacency of Europe.

And all the time we were getting wetter and wetter—while I kept hollering for an umbrella or wishing loudly and repeatedly that I had a pair of rubbers, and wanting more brandy. Thornton continued effervescent and euphoric, as if he were the one getting drunk—and then we had to search out the house where Nietzsche "in great loneliness" wrote *Also Sprach Zarathustra*.

I still called for an umbrella, but we had to stay up until dawn so that we could "hear the bells of Zurich, as Max Beerbohm described them"; and then finally, soaked through and thoroughly soused, I was steered back to my hotel by Thornton, where I fell into bed and slept until late that afternoon. He, meanwhile, went to his hotel and that morning wrote the whole of the last act of *Our Town*. It was not until I saw the play that I connected the umbrellas at the opening of that act with my yelling for one that wet night in Zurich. He had, as Gertrude told me later, "struck a match on me."

As for myself, at the moment I was vaguely remembering a short story I had read about an old man who had to have youth around him to feed on. Thornton was only twelve years older than myself, but it seemed more like thirty; he was a little too sweet and old-maidish for my contemporary "slickness."

During those several days he lectured me about my

74

homosexuality—which he had got me to confess early on—telling me how to handle it in a kind of four-way treatment (which was, perhaps, Thornton's own advice to himself): Think how to run your classes most easily without draining yourself; write some essays (why, in heaven's name?); consider your childhood and youth thoroughly, seeking out and examining all the disgusting things regarding sex until they are no longer repulsive; and study the lives and careers of the great homosexuals from the beginning down to the present day—Leonardo and Michelangelo to Whitman and beyond . . .

After this wordy intellectual preparation, sort of like tenderizing a tough cube steak, we climbed into bed together, myself half-drunk as I had to be in those days to have an encounter.

Thornton went about sex almost as if he were looking the other way, doing something else, and nothing happened that could be prosecuted anywhere, unless *frottage* can be called a crime. There was never even any kissing. On top of me, and after ninety seconds and a dozen strokes against my belly he ejaculated. At this he sprang from our bed of roses and exclaimed in his rapid way: "Didntyoucome? Didntyoucome?"

No, I didn't.

Thus began the casual acquaintance with Thornton Wilder that lasted through the war years and beyond, ending sometime in 1948. I became his Chicago piece, possibly his only physical contact in the city. If there were others I knew nothing of them, for there was a double-lock on the door of the closet in which he lived. Later in our acquaintance he let me understand by various oblique hints that he had sometimes been emotionally involved, but nothing was said directly. He could never forthrightly discuss anything sexual; for him the act itself was quite literally unspeakable. His puritan reluctance was inhibiting to me as well; I could not talk about such matters while I was with him, for he made such discussion seem somehow indecent, in bad taste. It was once, while saying how good-looking he thought Montgomery Clift to be, that he caught me regarding him rather quizzically. More for the satisfaction of my own curiosity than for knowing about Thornton, I wanted to ask about Clift who was also an attractive person to me.

"Have you—?" I began tentatively, and then stopped.

There was a brief silence. Then Thornton said, looking off into an upper corner of the room, "I am afraid—" and he chuckled nervously, "that in all of my male friendships there is always a touch of Eros."

He could not bring himself to say any more. But the sentence itself was revelatory; it opened speculation on many horizons, and many landscapes with figures.

Every time Thornton came to Chicago I would receive in advance a phone call or one of his chatty postcards, containing about two hundred words in his minuscule handwriting; and I would go down to the Stevens Hotel (now the Conrad Hilton) to spend the appointed night in Room 1000. On such nights he might show me his elaborately annotated copy of *Finnegans Wake*, the margins so black with his innumerable notes that there was hardly any white to be seen; or he would draw a score of Palestrina from his suitcase and tell me how he spent hours alone in hotel rooms "reading" the music to himself, enjoying it as much as if he were hearing it. And it kept him from cruising.

Occasionally he would come out to my northside apartment. Once he left his wristwatch on the night table beside the bed, and sent me a telegram the next day asking me to forward the watch to him in Arizona or else bring it to the hotel. The telegram was possibly one of the few bits of evidence he might have left that would have exposed his dread secret.

In Chicago there were two good friends to whom Gertrude Stein had originally introduced me by letter— Wendell and Esther Wilcox. Wendell was a writer, and in 1945 had had a novel published, *Everything is Quite All Right*. His great passion was the Latin poet Catullus about whom he planned to write a novel. But Wendell made the mistake of detailing his carefully researched plot to Thornton, and some time later Thornton's *The Ides of March* appeared. Therein, alas! Wendell found his plot.

After that Thornton discovered that many of his friends in Chicago disappeared or grew cool as the story about Catullus gained wider circulation. I was one of the friends who vanished.

One night in Paris in 1939 he had been to the theatre, and we met afterwards at the Café de la Paix. He said that he would walk me home to the Hôtel Récamier.

And so he did. As we went down the Avenue de l'Opéra, a female prostitute on the streetside plucked at his arm, importuning him to come with her, and falling into step beside us. He pulled his arm away and went on busily talking to me as if he had not seen or heard her. Not to be put off, the girl continued to pull at him. Finally he disengaged his arm, turning to her as if he had just then become aware of her existence.

"Not tonight, not tonight," he said, with an inflection suggesting that on any other night in the twentieth century he would have said yes. The girl went away and Thornton continued his euphoric monologue as if she had never been there at all.

And so he went through life, bright eyed and eager, interested in everything, talking, talking, looking away from the specter of sex that walked beside him, always hoping that it would disappear. But it never did.

And there was never, never, never a kiss . . .

Chapter V

THE MYSTIQUE OF THE TATTOO

L ET US IMAGINE THAT YOU are walking barefoot down a dusty country lane—hot and tired because the bastard made you get out of his Porsche when you refused to let him have his way with you. There is a glade to your left, and you leave the road. Soon you hear the splash and chuckle of a running stream—a waterfall?—and see ahead a sunny spot of greenery, and a pool.

But someone has got there before you. Through the leafy screen you see a naked body tanned to the waist; one knee is raised—he is stepping out of his trousers.

Full of Whitmanesque fancies, perhaps even seeing a Greek youth who has just come from the games, you allow yourself a dream. And then he turns so that you can see his left side. And what is that on his upper arm? A mark—a shadow—Good God! a tattoo!

There are two possible reactions. You may be completely fascinated, feeling that here is the ultimate stud, the great macho, the sylvan satyr, the Marlboro man, the far-traveling sailor, the incomparable sadistic master, the Genet criminal just released from prison. Or you may be just as completely revolted: seeing in him the epitome of sleaze, of low-class background, of cheap vulgarity and bad taste, of everything that with your intelligence and superior sophistication you have been conditioned to despise. You remember reading in an obscure 1930 novel about the signs of evil in an early anti-hero: socks carefully rolled down the calf of the leg to a point above the anklebone, sideburns that tapered to a point just short of the jaw line, and a tattoo coiled around the upper arm.

Tattooing has had a strange history, with many alternating periods of strong favor and intense loathing. Wars and depressions mark periods of its highest vogue. At one time in America it was associated only with the criminal classes—as indeed it was in France until about ten years ago when a shop was opened in Montmartre; before that the only tattoos were applied by hand-pricking in prison. In the early years of this century in America, even some of the "400" in the best circles of New York society wore them. The rise and fall of popularity in tattooing is charted in Albert Parry's *Tattoo*, a neo-Freudian study made in 1933 which is still largely relevant today.

After twenty years of university teaching, I gave it all up to become a tattoo artist. My friends and colleagues were deeply shocked; they could not understand my motivations. I tried to explain that I had grown to loathe teaching, that the students grew duller and more stupid year by year (I had found an entering freshman class, not one of whom had ever heard of Homer), and finally that the money was inadequate.

Their response in nearly every case was: "But *tattooing!*" as if it would have been nobler to clean urinals.

How could I go on to tell them that I wanted freedom, that it was a grand new way to feast the eyes on male beauty, that one could now touch the skin which you could only look at in the classroom—the arms, the legs, the chest—and there would be no one to raise an eyebrow, and even that you could in the right instances take a young man to the cot in the back room.

The motives were clear enough to me. The fact remains that I resigned from university teaching and became a tattoo artist in Chicago, working under the needle-name of Phil Sparrow—which I had lifted from John Skelton's fifteenth-century poem, *The Boke of Phyllyp Sparowe*, a lady's lament for the death of her pet sparrow which used to pick crumbs from her cleavage.

But as a university professor of English, I knew nothing about the means and methods of tattooing. How to learn this arcane and mysterious art? A small nutty fellow named Larry, himself tattooed heavily all over his body, told me that a wino in a flophouse, an ex-tattoo artiste, wanted to sell a footlocker filled with acetate stencils, old pigment-encrusted machines, and some "flash"—designs to be hung on the walls. I bought the smelly stuff for thirty-five dollars.

Then I purchased a correspondence course in tattooing from some con artist in Rockford, Illinois—and learned next to nothing from its pages. Becoming a tattoo artist that way was like trying to learn to swim from a book in your living room, so I went to Milwaukee and plunked a few dollars down in front of one of the grand old masters of the art—Amund Dietzel. From him in two hours I got more than from all the twenty-five lessons in the correspondence course.

Then I began, guided by Larry (my Virgil through the Inferno) to State Street's skidrow and the Playland Arcade. And at Dr. Kinsey's request I started a journal on the sexual motivations of tattooing, in 1965 moving to California where I worked for another five years, making a total of eighteen in the racket.

Early in the experience an anonymous letter came to me, so significantly related to the mystique of the "observed" tattoo that part of it should be quoted:

Dear Phil,

I stood and watched you for a long time the other night. You had a lot of sailors in your shop. I think you must have the most romantic occupation in the world. You come closer to them than anybody. Doesn't it give you a feeling of domination over them to tattoo them? Don't you feel that the Sailor thereafter carries around with Him, to the end of His days, your Mark upon Him? . . . If He flinches, are you not His master? Is He not the Slave, bearing your mark?

Or from another angle, does not the Sailor thereafter carry with Him your own creation beneath His skin? Do you not symbolically go with Him to the far places, the far suns and seas, the bamboo huts of savages and the stone lacework of Indian castles, the crystal pools and sands of Persia, white columns against the dark blue Greek skies, the golden suns and fountains of red-walled Rome? Can you not know a little, then, of a way of life which is denied to most of us? Do you not . . . actually accompany the Sailor on His far wanderings? Are you not part of Him, flesh of His flesh? When, panting and naked, He braces Himself between her legs, do you not ride high on His shoulder in the design you applied there? Or are you not crushed between His brave and swelling pectorals and her flattened breast? Or ride the bucking-horse from the peak-point of His pelvic bone? . . . And did He not receive you with His blood? Are you not coupled with Him in a mystic vow of comradeship . . . a gypsy blood-brother oath that you have taken with Him? . . .

and so on, for another page. Kinsey was especially interested not only in the evident masochism of the writer, but in the fact that he had capitalized all words relating to the sailor, as if he were a holy object.

In the early part of my experience with tattooing, before the leather movement began in the middle 1950s, there were very few homosexuals getting tattooed. I kept a running count of the overt or obvious ones who got a tattoo in those first years, with some interesting results: out of the first fifty thousand tattoos, only forty-three were put on recognized homosexuals. This led to a great deal of headshaking between Kinsey and myself, and to a conclusion that narcissism played a large part in one's decision about a tattoo. Since narcissism is one of the important elements of homosexuality, it might follow that many homosexuals did not want to spoil their pretty pink bodies with a tattoo, being satisfied with themselves as they were. Lines of questioning revealed their reasons for disinclination: one said "I can't imagine myself being permanently satisfied with one design—I'd be wanting to change it after a little while." Another was sure he couldn't stand the pain, and a young Chicago elegant said: "Really, m'dear, it's too low-class for words. I couldn't stoop that low." (Just for the record, he turned out to be a coprophage, but that doesn't matter.) Still another in a Brooks Brothers suit said that he had always rejected frills and decorations—in his clothes and his life in

81

general, and therefore naturally he disapproved of such fripperies as tattoos. And finally, one perceptive person said that he was afraid of the revelation a tattoo might make of his sexual inclinations.

Thus very early I discovered how impossible it was to consider a tattoo on a person objectively. You see one—and immediately you associate it—and the wearer—with some area of your past experience, pleasant or unpleasant, sexual or antisocial. The mystique of the tattoo becomes as highly subjective a matter as one's personal idea of what constitutes beauty. You are either turned on or off according to your background and associations. Consequently, generalizations about tattoos are extremely dangerous and unreliable. Your reaction to a tattoo is established only by the fashion in which your own emotions and observations, your backgrounds and personality are fused together.

There is a wide gulf of difference between a "tattoo observed" and a "tattoo worn" on the skin. In the journal I kept for Kinsey—which totaled close to a million words in eight years—I noted thirty-two motivations for getting tattooed, of which twenty-five were sexual in whole or part. The remaining seven were of small interest, being utilitarian (social security numbers, blood types), ethnic (shamrocks for Ireland), anniversary markers, and such like.

Of the group with sexual motivations, by far the most heavily weighted reason for getting one was an assertion of masculine status, so much so that early on I made a sign for my shop which said: "Depressed? Downhearted? A good tattoo may make you feel like a man again."

The sign led me to some thinking to try to discover what might have been wrong with the young American male, and I finally concluded that the concept of the Hero had been removed. It had disappeared in three ways, and the young were searching for it again.

The destruction of the Hero had begun with the advance of equal rights for women and the gradual shift of the country towards the permissiveness of a matriarchy—all of which had been bitterly chronicled as early as the 1930s when Philip Wylie investigated the idea of Momism.

82

Women had encroached on what had previously been the exclusive territory of the male. Again, the concept of the Hero as Breadwinner was slowly being challenged not only by the rivalry of women in the marketplace but by the growth of automation, machines, and computers. Finally, the idea of the Hero as Warrior had been destroyed. Man with his bow and arrows, shotguns, and TNT bombs had been ruined by the development of nuclear fusion and fission—for what warrior was brave enough to fight the little killing sun of Hiroshima? And what good would it do if he were?

A tattoo, then, helped to underline one's masculine status. How male an ineffectual little pipsqueak could feel as he looked into the mirror at the new tattoo that first night and masturbated, certain that he was at last a Man! Recorder that I was, I kept a tally of persons who returned for a second tattoo, casually probing their reactions to the first one. I asked some questions in phrasings like: "Well, did you enjoy your first tattoo? Lotsa guys tell me they went out and got fucked, or got in a fight, or got drunk, or jacked off in front of a mirror. What did you do?"

Many, of course, simply laughed and made no reply at all, but certain totals appeared after about five years: Those who got laid, 1724; in a fight, 635; who got drunk (over 800 of those of the first question also said they got drunk), 231; those who masturbated in front of a mirror, 879. Even after making allowances for braggadocio, the proportions between the figures were interesting.

I found the close corollary of narcissism to be exhibitionism. People always seemed to want to show off their tattoos. If I happened to ask a prospective customer if he were already tattooed, there would rarely be a simple "yes" for an answer. The sleeves would be rolled up, the jacket removed, or the pants dropped to show what he had—in the way of tattoos, that is. Curiously, it took two or three years for me to find out why so many young men had their first tattoo on the left biceps rather than the right. If it were on the left arm, that arm could be hung out the window while driving a car, to impress the girls. Or boys.

A handsome young Italian ex-con once dropped into the shop for no other reason except to inform me he had writing all over his cock.

"So?" I said with a hard inflection, *not* inviting him to show it to me.

"Yeah," he said. "I done it all in the pokey," wherewith he whipped it out. It was literally covered with very crudely done self-applied black writing. There was a small cherry with the usual words around it: "Here's mine—where's yours?" and in addition: "God's gift to women" as well as "Let me slide this long stiff pole into you."

"Well," I said, baffled to think of a comment, "there's not room for much more."

That remark insulted him because he thought I was speaking of the size of his dingdong, and he left.

Occasionally both narcissism and exhibitionism came together, as in the case of a guy from New York who ended with five large designs on his chest and arms. He confided that every morning when he saw himself in his full-length mirror, or while he was shaving, he had to masturbate because the tattoos excited him so much. He was extremely good-looking, a leatherboy who played the harp (!) and all the guys were after him; but after teasing them in the bars he would almost always go home alone to masturbate, home to his huge glittering concert-sized harp dripping with goldleaf grapes and baroque scrolls and rococo garbage—unless by chance he found a kindred soul to join him in his childhood games.

Then there was a thin white-skinned architectural drafts-man from Indiana, using only the name of Andrew and never telling me his last name, who wanted to get covered from neck to waistline. He came into my shop every three weeks for nearly a year, getting his back and torso covered with a profusion of macaws, swordfish, clipper ships, scarlet and gold petals around the blackened center of his nipples, spiders with webs in his armpits, snakes wrapped around his arms, panthers, and a very large peacock on his back—quite a colorful fellow when I had finished. Whether such decorations ever satisfactorily answered his deep desire to be a man, one could not know; and whether he performed better in bed with his partners—or let them go unfulfilled while he dallied with himself—is, like the song the mermaids sang, or the name Achilles assumed when he hid himself among the women, a puzzling matter but not one beyond all conjecture.

After about 1956 there was a noticeable change in the number of homosexuals getting tattooed. When the "leather movement" began, their numbers rapidly increased. Most of the tattoos on the s/m crowd were masculine symbols— tigers, panthers, daggers entwined with snakes. Oddly, they were placed mostly on those who were predominantly masochistic, and these persons stood the pain very well, whereas the "real" sadists often fainted.

Of the many homosexuals who fooled me for a while, there was Ed, a sailor from Great Lakes Naval Training Station. Because of some defect in his skin, or because of the laundry he had to do as a "boot" (thus wetting the tattoo too much while it was healing), the first coloring of his rose did not take well. He came back to have it recolored. Then he disappeared for four years during his Navy hitch. When he returned just before his discharge he had a great many tattoos. He came in the last time with a buddy of his, and in a double scroll under a flower he asked for the names Ed and Chuck. They had successfully been lovers in the Navy for four years without having been discovered. Ed proudly showed me the decorations on his cock which he had got in the Orient—a small "6" and "9" on the underside of the glans, separated by the frenum, a delicate octopus on the ventral side of the shaft and several other tiny designs.

A young Polish homosexual aged about nineteen brought in a curious design for his arm. It was an outline drawing of two men kissing, but their profiles had melted into each other so that the nose of each was in the center of the other's head. At first I objected, saying that he was advertising his preference and might some day regret it. "What would your mother say?" I asked. "She'd know at once you were gay."

"Oh, she already knows," he said. "She don't care. Matter of fact, she said that my goin' out with boys saved her a lotta

85

money, and was cheaper'n givin' me the bread to take girls out."

There were other examples of advertising, some subtle, some direct. On the buns of one young man I once printed "Screw" on the left side and "Me" on the right, with appropriate arrows. On another I put a rose tree, the idea having come to this particular hustler from a fake photograph he had seen: the rose tree began in the cleft of the ass near the anus, branched out onto the gluteus, and gracefully wandered up the spine with flowers here and there, branching finally into two divisions at the shoulders, each ending high on the peak of a deltoid. It was a charming *divertissement* for those who screwed him.

Another hustler "model" who operated in northern California had a snake's head about an inch below his navel, with the body of the snake curling down and under his scrotum and the tail coming up the other side. He later said that he was glad he got it because "no one ever forgets me once they see that design." Tattoos do have their place in the business world.

Possibly in all the years of tattooing the most frequently asked question I heard was "Does it hurt?" It was usually followed by: "Have you ever tattooed anyone's cock?"

There are only two professions in the world in which one man can hold another's genitalia in his hand and not be considered queer. One is that of physician, the other tattoo artist. A conservative estimate of the number of times I put tattoos on cocks is about five hundred. When you consider that in the years of tattooing I put on about 150,000 tattoos (quite a few acres of skin), 500 amounts to about only one-third of one percent.

You could easily tell when someone wanted a tattoo on his cock. There was a lot of hemming and hawing and much sidling about the room, until finally the customer would come out with a question about whether I would tattoo "any place" on the body.

A small sailor asked me that question in the second week of my "career," and I was almost as nervous as he was for I sensed what he meant. Then he said he would like to have a small heart at the base of his penis with a ring going clear around it, so that it would look like a finger ring set with a heart-shaped stone.

"What do you want with a design like that?" I asked, curious.

He almost giggled. "So that I'll always have a heart-on," he said.

I set about the preparation of his penis, having closed the shop and set up a screen. The penis is usually flaccid (unless you have a real masochist to deal with) because the client is frightened nearly out of his wits. He need not be. When the penis is soft the sensitivity of it is much diminished, save for the glans. And most of the cock tattoos were on the shaft, which has a quality of flesh quite different from that of the glans. The corpus cavernosum is not overly sensitive nor does it bleed as much as the glans—which produces such a gush that the pigments are washed away and the design has to be gone over several times.

The sailor who wanted the ring was nervous and so was I. In order to tattoo the penis one has to grasp it tightly on the sides with thumb and second finger, pulling down with them while pushing up on the urethral canal with the index finger; the skin must be taut or the needle will not penetrate.

I was quite as surprised as the sailor to see the reaction of the penis when the needle approached. It almost turned to jelly; it was endowed with a life of its own, seemingly— much to our astonishment. As the needle drew near, the organ jumped first one way and then the other, shrinking and trying to draw back into the belly in completely involuntary and uncontrollable movements.

On many other occasions, however, the organ remained hard, suggesting that the customer was either a crypto-masochist or a fully developed one. Many times ejaculations occurred while work was in progress, even on an arm or a shoulder.

There was one ugly pudgy little truckdriver who came into my Chicago shop once, finally getting up nerve enough to ask if I tattooed "any place." When I said yes, he told me that he had many tattoos in the groin region, but wanted one small space beneath the glans tattooed with a small flower.

He exposed himself behind the screen; his whole lower abdomen was covered with busts of girls, naked breasts showing, all facing towards the center of the pubic region. On the penis itself hardly a square millimeter was vacant—flowers, bees, writing, girls' small faces. On the underside of the shaft was an anchor.

"Right here," he said, indicating a spot to the left of the frenum. He stood for a moment, weighing his penis in his hand. "Sure looks purty, don't it?"

"Oh, very," I said, unshockable to the end.

"Sure proves I ain't queer, don't it? All them gurls."

"Oh, yeah," I said, thinking thoughts about insecurity and masculine status and cryptohomosexuality.

"It's fun in the whorehouse," he said. "The gals take it in their hand and say 'Oh, Flo—come lookit this.' "

I went to work on him, paying little attention to the fact that he was tumesced and lubricating, since by then I had done many cock designs.

Suddenly with a gasp he ejaculated all over everything.

"Chee, Phil," he said. "I'm sorry. Guess my imagination was workin' overtime."

I threw a couple of pieces of kleenex over him. "Well," I said, "you might as well relax and enjoy it."

After the ejaculation he lost interest in the tattoo. "You can let it go just as it is," he said, looking down at the half-finished job.

"Not on your life," I said. "You lie back down and get it finished."

He did, with much grumbling. This part of it hurt him like hell, since he was satisfied after he got his kicks. But I finished it. He never came back.

On the penises I have tattooed I have put many different designs, some of them amusing—such as the boy who wanted a thermometer on his, with red fluid showing in the tube "so's I can take the temperature of the holes I go into." One penis was colored entirely green; another was scaled green to look like a snake, with mouth, eyes, and fangs on the head—which was itself colored red and yellow. The most common cock-design was a small fly, or a small fish for "those who can't eat meat on Friday" before the Catholic church changed its rules.

One of the most fascinating penile tattoos was done on a sailor who wanted the two words, "Your" and "Name," on the shaft. Later he returned to tell me why.

"I ain't bought a drink in a bar since you did that," he said, and described his *modus operandi*. "What I do, see, is go in a bar and sit down beside some guy who's about half-smashed, and then after a coupla minutes I say to him 'Say, I betcha I got your name tattooed on my cock,' and that allus jolts him and he says 'Like hell—we just met,' and I go on sayin' I betcha and finally he bets five bucks and we go back to the head and I shows him, and sure enough there it says 'Your Name' and I got five bucks to drink on." He looked thoughtful a moment, and sighed. "Trouble is," he said, "I'm runnin' outa bars. I can't do it but oncet in one place."

I saw a lot of self-applied tattooing in my shop, most of it done in the prisons of America. Such a pastime was much frowned on by the authorities, but that did not keep it from being popular. The trick was to steal three small needles from the tailor shop, bind them tightly with thread, and for "ink" burn and crumble toilet paper and mix it with water or saliva, or burn a candle against the cement ceiling and collect the soot. Then the two cellmates would climb under a blanket with needles, ink, and a flashlight and proceed to tattoo each other. The proximity of their naked bodies and the heat generated—plus the "illegal" excitement of tattooing—in nearly every case generated a sexual arousal, ending in mutual masturbation, fellatio, anal intercourse or other boyish delights. Stories of such experiences were told me dozens of times by ex-convicts who came in to have their "pokey" designs covered with professional work.

In Chicago in the 1950s there were but few women tattooed. Occasionally a lesbian would wander in, or a prostitute, or a farm-wife from downstate Illinois who knew no better. One whore wanted a swallowtail butterfly, with one tail down each side of the celestial gate.

I pulled downwards with my fingertips on each side of the

portal, but could not manage to get the skin taut enough to get the color in. Finally in desperation I said, "You'll just have to excuse me," and therewith inserted two fingers and pushed outwards. The pigments went in wonderfully well. All she said, with a small squirm, was "Nnnnnh..."

In the 1950s an estimate of five females to ninety-five males would be about right for the percentages getting tattooed in my shop. Nowadays the proportions seem to have changed, and the percentages to have violently altered, although if one is measuring the acres of skin covered, the men still win out by far. But for numbers of bodies crossing the tattoo thresholds the women equal the men, or perhaps surpass them slightly; however, the women (mostly lesbian, with masculine slant) get only very small designs—a heart on the breast in the Janis Joplin style, a small flower, a trailing vine of blossoms—something lacy and fragile-looking, although some want larger designs in the Mucha-Art-Nouveau tradition.

About 1968 in California I was discovered by the Hells (no apostrophe) Angels. This group of aging rebels suddenly found that in my shop they could get their symbols—the winged skull with "Hells Angels" written curving above it and chapter name beneath—for about one-third of what they would have to pay elsewhere. The word flashed around, as it had earlier with the youth gangs in Chicago; and in a sense I became for a while the "official" tattoo artist for their groups. They came from all parts of California, eventually, even as far away as San Bernardino, led by their "prez" Sonny Barger. Not only did they want the skull with wings, but other designs which were arcane and esoteric—at least until the Angels started getting all their publicity. They got swastikas and iron crosses, the jagged "SS" symbol, the 1% (someone had said only 1% of all motorcyclists were outlaws). They got pilot's wings—brown to mean they had screwed a man, red for cunnilingus on a menstruating old lady, or black—the same on a black woman. Or they got "13" for the letter "M" (13th down the alphabet) meaning marijuana, "DFFL"—Dope Forever, Forever Loaded; 666—the number of the beast in the

Apocalypse, since a preacher had called them that—and other symbols transient in meaning.

But even the Angels had inner circles: a few got specialized symbols. I will not forget my astonishment when Sonny Barger got a long philosophical quotation from (I think) Khalil Gibran on his inner right forearm beginning: "I had rather die yearning..."

At first the Angels were terrifying but then gradually I acquired a kind of special status so that I could indulge in kidding and badinage with them, whereas the same words from a stranger would have resulted in a broken jaw. After all, since I held the needle I was boss . . . for the moment.

A sample bit: judging by the remarks of the others, one of the Angels reputedly had the biggest schwanz in the Bay Area. One night while they were talking about it, I took out a small rubber fingerstall such as doctors use when palpating the prostate. It was rolled into a condom but was only half an inch in diameter.

"Here," I said, tossing it at him, "take this and go have a wild time tonight."

The others roared; he raised his arm against me, but I ducked and laughed. I must either have been sure of myself or very foolhardy.

The Angels were very jealous of their symbols, which they called "colors." One evening I had closed the shop and gone home when there came a call about midnight from Sonny Barger.

"Can you come down and open up again for a special job?" he asked.

"Jaysus, Sonny," I protested. "It's late and I just got home."

"It's important," he said. "Can you come?"

Grudgingly I said yes and rode the bus from Berkeley back to Oakland. There were four or five Angels in front of the shop, and they had in their grip a banged-up young man with a black eye and bloody nose.

"He's got our tattoo on his arm," one of them explained, "and he ain't no Angel."

"We want it covered up," another explained. "Blacked out

completely.''

"Hold on a minute," I said, opening the shop. "Technically this is mayhem. Tattooing under duress. He'll have to sign a release," I wrote one out in a hurry, stating that he wanted the tattoo blacked out. "Is that true?" I asked him.

The frightened young man gulped and nodded and signed with trembling fingers. I blacked out the design, with each of the Angels taking turns in jabbing the needle into the skin. Afterwards they threw the young man into a small enclosed truck and climbed in after him.

I heard later that they drove him into the country, knocked him around some more, sodomized him and stripped him naked, and dropped him on the freeway.

Despite all the news articles and studies by neo-Freudian psychologists about the Hells Angels, the fact remains that they were tough and mean and had to be handled with care. I had a distinct admiration for Ralph Barger—an intelligent person, cool and thoughtful. When the occasion demanded he could be as clean-cut and well-shaved an American male as you would want to see, even handsome in those days.

Perhaps to the present moment I might still be sitting in the Anchor Tattoo Shop in dingy Oakland, fiddling with soldering needles and mixing pigments and bullshitting customers were it not that I was strong-armed and robbed three times in the shop by our black brothers. I decided that a fourth time might mean a bullet or a knife, instead of a thick black arm around my neck while a black hand fumbled for my wallet. I closed the shop forever in 1970.

There are many more motivations, and a considerable mystique, to tattooing—such things as pseudo-narcissism, "pure" decoration, the herd instinct, possession, rivalry, manhood initiation rites, existential motives, compensation, compulsion, "aliveness," and others which would be interesting only to psychological investigators or to persons like Kinsey.

Albert Parry's assertion in *Tattoo* that the act of tattooing is in many ways similar to the sexual act has something in its favor, although it is somewhat farfetched. He pointed out that in tattooing there was an active partner (the artist), a passive one (the customer), the injection of fluid into the skin, and so forth. Such statements may be fanciful, but Parry does not mention one notable thing: a kind of temporary love affair between artist and customer. If conditions are precisely right, and no one else is in the shop, the customer's defenses fall as soon as the needle starts to work; and he tells the artist things which (I am sure) he has never told his wife or girlfriend or best buddy. The tattoo artist becomes for him a psychiatrist, priest, best boyfriend, mother, father—a kind of "blood confessor," and for a little while one can almost notice a lingering incense as the dingy shop becomes a sort of shadowed confessional.

There is no denying the high sexual mystique of a tattoo for many persons. One cold snowy evening in Chicago a sailor came into my shop all alone and got his first tattoo: an anchor on his forearm. After it was finished and bandaged, he asked if there were a head in the place. I told him where the toilet was, and he went back to it.

He was gone a little too long to urinate and not long enough for something more weighty. Moreover, when he came back, waved goodbye and left, I was struck by one curious thing: I had not heard the toilet flush.

I went back to investigate. The sailor had masturbated and spread the still-steaming ejaculate all over the cold cement floor.

Tattooing, although it flourishes during depressions and wars, has always had America's basic puritanism ranged against it. It has been considered faintly evil, criminal, and nasty. Right Wingers and Little Old Ladies denounce it, seeing it as the *cause* of criminal behavior or believing it to be prohibited by religion (it is in orthodox Judaism, but only there). They are incapable of realizing that—if convicts and murderers happen to have tattoos—the damage was done before the tattoo was applied. A tattoo does not turn a man into a criminal any more than it turns him into a saint. But for the puritans of the world, tattooing is strange, dark, and evil, a mysterious subculture, and should therefore be outlawed.

It is, of course, no such thing. But the aura of mystery

remains. Tattooing is merely the last of the unchanged folk arts, a highly lucrative calling for the exceptionally skillful practitioners, and the most superb substitute for cruising that ever has been invented. If you become a tattoo artist, you will never have to go searching into the bars or the baths again, for then you will find, as I did, that . . .

. . . all the beauties will come looking for you . . .

Chapter VI

DOCTOR PROMETHEUS

PERHAPS IT IS APPROPRIATE to offer a small wreath to the work of Dr. Alfred C. Kinsey. It would be too much to say that the Stonewall riots in 1969—a landmark of rebellion in the gay movement—would have been impossible without his pioneer studies; but had he not lived and labored it would perhaps have been necessary to invent him. Many of the younger persons of the "Me Generation" seem barely aware of his animating Promethean efforts, but he truly brought fire and light to the world in 1948 with his findings about homosexuality and the sexual *mores* of the American male. Freud as intuitive creator, Havelock Ellis as arranger and synthesizer, and Kinsey as scientist and investigator accomplished the liberating enlightenment of our century regarding sex.

Not long ago a young man of about twenty-three came to interview me, arriving under the banner of one of the numerous superficial sex research surveys being done every other day in the San Francisco area. During the course of the usual dull questions the matter of previous surveys came up. He mentioned Masters and Johnson, and I scoffed somewhat at their ridiculously scanty sampling of 176 homosexuals, comparing it unfavorably with Kinsey's totals of 12,000 men and 6,000 women.

At that point he said: "Who's Kinsey?"

I recovered from that jolt with difficulty, finding it incredible that a sex-survey interviewer should never have heard of a man who left a deep imprint on nearly everything said and done in the psychology of sex since the late 1940s. But for all too many persons today the world began with the day of their birth; what went before is of no importance to them.

It was my privilege to know Kinsey fairly well during the last eight years of his life. In 1949 I was teaching English at my second-rate sectarian university in Chicago when I made the acquaintance of a guy in the speech department named Theodore, who came to me one day in the shabby halls and asked without preamble: "How would you like to meet Doctor Alfred C. Kinsey?"

I was flabber and gasted. "Good heavens," I said, "you don't mean to say you know him!"

He nodded. "Long time," he said. "Matter of fact, I was the one to help him get started interviewing in Chicago."

This was just after the publication of *Sexual Behavior in the Human Male* when Kinsey's star was high and his name was on everyone's lips. Comics made jokes about him, he was constantly being interviewed, and the world was trembling with his revelations about the prevalence of male homosexuality in the United States, and equally agog in anticipation of his sequel volume on the female.

So Theodore arranged it and Doctor Kinsey came to my apartment. The interview would last an hour, Theodore said, although sometimes they ran longer if the interviewee had a lot to say.

I opened the door to a solidly built man in his fifties wearing a rumpled grey suit. He had a friendly face. His greying buff-colored hair stood in a short unruly pompadour; his eyes were sometimes blue and sometimes hazel. He had a rather sensitive but tense wide mouth above a somewhat bulldog or prognathous jaw, which in turn jutted out above his ever-present bow tie.

Indeed, Theodore had been a bit misinformed. The interview lasted five hours, and it seemed to me that I answered thousands of questions—although there were in reality only a few hundred. The thing that amazed him most of all was that he found I was a "recordkeeper"—something all too rare, he said. But I had an accurate count on the number of persons I had been to bed with, the total number of times of "releases" (as he termed them) with other persons, number of repeats, and all the usual statistical information, taken from the "Stud File" that I had kept on three-by-five cards from my very first contact many years before in Ohio. My information like Kinsey's was coded, but not so unbreakably or exhaustively. I showed him the file; he was fascinated. At the end of the interview he looked at me thoughtfully and said, "Why don't you give up trying to continue your heterosexual relationships?"

I abandoned my phony "bisexuality" that very evening. Poor Emmy.

The interview marked the beginning of a friendship that lasted until his death from overwork in 1956. I became one of the "unofficial collaborators" for the Institute for Sex Research. In the days when he was still alive, no one could officially work for the Institute who was not of the "majority sexual orientation"; all his associates had to be married, preferably with children, or else be absolutely asexual. He felt that otherwise the reliability and objectivity of the research might be tainted or compromised.

Unofficially, then, I steered people to him or him to people, gave him samples of my literary production ranging from sentimental sex stories written in highschool to a translation done as a labor of love of Genet's *Querelle de Brest*, and a "dirty" novel of mine that was too much even for Jack Kahane in Paris in 1938 when he had the Obelisk Press. I deposited in the archives dozens of typewritten stories that used to circulate in such form before the explosion of pornography in 1966. And I gave him all the artwork I had done (he used to give me duplicate photographs from his collection which I would turn into line drawings in the Cocteau manner, or make watercolor washes thereof). I also turned over to him the chapter of my doctoral dissertation in which I had discovered Cardinal Newman's homosexuality, as well as the sexual-action Polaroid pictures I had taken in the early 1950s when those cameras first made their appearance. The polaroids, like bread cast upon the waters, came back to me eventually in a more beautiful form—eight-by-ten photographs blown up and reproduced by Kinsey's official photographer, Bill Dellenback. I managed to find copies of my two early books, *Pan and the Firebird* and *Angels on the Bough*, to add to the library. Later on, at their request, I sent the Institute all of the Phil Andros novels I had produced, together with a bibliography locating the hundred and fifty stories I had written for European and other magazines, and all the ephemera and reproduced artwork I had done.

Kinsey favored me in return with the most flattering kind of attention—never coming to Chicago without writing to me in advance to arrange a meeting. In the eight years of our friendship I logged (as a recordkeeper again) about seven hundred hours of his pleasant company, the most fascinating in the world because all his shoptalk was of sex—and what is more interesting than that? He taught me some of their "little language," the shorthand speech which he and his associates used, so that at lunch or dinner in public places they could still discuss the most hair-raising matters—"h" for homosexual, "ht" for heterosexual, "s/m" for sadomasochistic (one he originated that spread widely), "tv' for transvestite, and several others. Thus one of the group might say: "My history today liked Go better than Z, but Ag with an H really made him er," each letter being pronounced separately. Translation: "My history today liked genital-oral contact better than that with animals, but anal-genital with a homosexual really turned him on."

In those early years he had one of the warmest personalities I had ever met—a cordial gregarious man as approachable as an old park bench, and just as much of an accomplished con-artist as I was later to become in my tattoo career. The "con" approach was deliberately cultivated by him, so that he could win the trust of the person being interviewed; in like manner, he took up smoking and drinking (very, very gingerly) to put his interviewees at ease. His warmth and approachability were further improved by his talent for talking to the most uneducated hustlers and prostitutes and pimps in their own language, no matter how coarse. It gained trust for him among the suspicious ones, and word of his honesty and secrecy opened doors for him that would have remained closed forever to a more academic attitude.

I learned many things from him, and in a sense some

degree of "transference" took place in me. Though there was a difference of only about fifteen years in our ages, after the initial interview he became for me a sort of father-figure as he did for so many. Several women said, innocently enough, that they had been frigid until interviewed by Kinsey. In him I saw the ideal father—who was never shocked, who never criticized, who always approved, who listened and sympathized. I suppose that to a degree I fell in love with him, even though he was a grandfather. Of course there was never any physical contact between us except a handshake. Many persons would ask me: "Is he queer?"

I told him this. "And what do you answer?" he asked.

"Well," I said slowly, "I always say 'Yes, he is—but not in the same way we are. He is a *voyeur* and an *auditeur*. He likes to look and listen.' "

Kinsey laughed, but a moment later I caught him observing me thoughtfully. I may have hit closer to the truth than I realized.

I learned also never again in my life to use the word "normal," which I once thoughtlessly employed in front of him. He jumped on me. "Just what do you mean?" he said. "Usual? Usual for whom—you, me, the rest of the world?" and he scolded me roundly. From that moment the word was sliced from my vocabulary, and replaced with something more exact, but clumsier, such as "majority practice." But I partly redeemed myself by quoting Gide's phrase for him, which he had not heard until then, the one about "your normal is my abnormal."

And little acts were also corrected. Once while I was visiting him in Bloomington we went to lunch and stopped in a men's room first, to take a leak. Afterwards I washed my hands.

"Why did you do that?" he asked.

Somewhat confused, I said, "I guess because I was brought up that way—to wash my hands after handling myself."

"Ah *hah!*" he said triumphantly. "A victim of the Judeo-Christian ethos of the Old Testament! Don't you realize that it would be much more sensible to wash your hands *before* handling yourself? The Old Testament says you'll be unclean 'until the even' if you touch yourself. But think of today's door handles, and all the other things you've touched during the past four hours."

Again, at lunch at the Indiana University Union, as I think it was called, there was a small container of monosodium glutamate on the table. I sprinkled some on a fingertip and touched it to my tongue.

"Did you ever notice," I said thoughtfully to the table at large, at which were seated Kinsey, Wardell Pomeroy, and Paul Gebhard, "how closely the taste of monosodium glutamate resembles that of semen?"

There was a moment of dead silence, and the enormity of my *gaffe* turned me rosy as I slowly realized that I had spoken to three presumably straight heterosexuals.

Kinsey grinned. "I do believe," he said, "that not a single one of us here has ever noticed the similarity, but your remark will be noted for future reference."

Everyone laughed. "I thought," I said, "that certainly this time I might trap someone into admitting he was a club member."

He grinned. "I mustn't say. We must preserve the confidentiality of the research."

When the time came for the appearance of the volume on females, we chuckled over his statement in the introduction that since the orgasm lasted only seconds, it had been necessary to film the act; and that the Institute had in its archives filmed records of the orgasms of fourteen species of mammals—the amusing part being that in 1953 the Indiana University regents could still be shocked—and that somewhere among the fourteen was of course the human animal. Similarly, we enjoyed the insertion into the female volume of perhaps one of the most detailed and thorough expositions of the technique of erotic arousal and contact, a genuine *ars amatoria* or *Kama Sutra*, to be seen up to that time in English.

Kinsey from the very beginning gave me free access to the archives and library of the Institute—which even in 1950 was rapidly catching up with—nay, overtaking—the fabled Vatican collection of pornography. At the present time the Institute's collection of erotica—literary and artistic—is much larger than that of the Vatican. And into this "gorgeous Gallery of Gallant Inventions," this "Paradyse of Daintie Devices," the light-bringer to mankind, Doctor Prometheus (né Kinsey), turned me loose, to ramble and enjoy and feast to surfeit. Each time I went to Bloomington I saw a thousand new things I had not seen before.

"Turned me loose," however, is not quite an exact phrase. The security and the protection of the materials at the Institute was intense. On the first tour Kinsey gave me, I noted that our progress was considerably slowed by the fact that each door had to be unlocked to enter, and then re-locked behind us. The interview material, contained in an elaborate mark-and-placement code which Kinsey had invented, was carefully guarded. The code itself took about a year to learn, and had been submitted to the best crypt-analysts of the military—who all pronounced it unbreakable unless the secret of the positioning could be learned. To protect the material further, only about four persons knew the code; if they were to be together at the same time in, say, California, each had to take a different plane, so that the code would always survive an air disaster.

Kinsey and I had known each other about a year when he proposed an "arrangement" to me. He was extremely scrupulous about the confidentiality of his "subjects" and never set up assignations of any kind—but his interest in sadomasochism had reached a point of intolerable tension. He knew that I had experimented in that arena and he wanted to find out more. This was in 1949, long before the leather mania had codified and ritualized itself into leather-drag posturings, studied gestures, codes of dress and behavior that Genet had partially described and ana-lyzed earlier in *Querelle de Brest*.

He therefore asked me to fly down from Chicago, and from New York he invited a tall mean-looking sadist, Mike Miksche, with a crewcut and a great personality. Mike was a freelance artist, doing fashion layouts for Saks and other Fifth Avenue stores; and under the name of Steve Masters (S.M.) he produced many homosexual ink-drawings for the growing s/m audience. We were to be filmed in an encounter.

It was quite an experience. For two afternoons at Bloomington the camera whirred away. Kinsey prepared Mike by getting him half-drunk on gin—an advantage for him but a disadvantage for me, since I had stopped drinking and could no longer join him in his happy euphoria. Sitting under an apple tree in Kinsey's garden before the festivities began, the Imp of the Perverse made me look down at one of Miksche's stylish brown English riding-boots (black had not yet become the leather-boys' standard color) that had a bit of lacing at the instep. I plucked at one end of the lace and untied it, saying, "Humph—you don't look so tough to me."

That was a deliberate challenge, of course, for which I paid dearly again and again during the next two afternoons. Mike was quite a ham actor; every time he heard Bill Dellenback's camera start to turn, he renewed his vigor and youth like the green bay tree; and at the end of the second afternoon I was exhausted, marked and marred, all muscles weakened. During the sessions I was vaguely conscious of people dropping in now and then to observe, while Mrs. Kinsey—a true scientist to the end—sat by, and once in a while calmly changed the sheets upon the workbench.

At the end of the last session, when my jaws were so tired and unhinged that I could scarcely close my mouth, let alone hold a cigarette between my lips, Mike got really angry and slapped me hard on each cheek, saying that I was the lousiest cocksucker he had ever seen. I could have killed him at that moment. I sprang from the bed and ran to the shower; he followed me, but I was still seething. Later that evening Kinsey left Mike and me in separate parts of the library to do some reading; and suddenly Mike appeared, wild-fire-eyed and excited—having stimulated himself with some typewritten s/m stories—and had his way with me on the cold cement floor of the library stacks.

102

When Kinsey heard of the encounter, he laughed and said, "I hope the blinds were closed."

Mike Miksche later bore out the theorizing of Theodore Reik, Wilhelm Stekel, and Kinsey himself that sadists were perhaps not as well-balanced as masochists, for Mike—after attempting and failing to turn his directions to heterosexuality by getting married—jumped into the Hudson River one winter day and committed suicide. His great talents as an artist and his good intellect were lost to the world too soon.

Kinsey had two interests aside from his all-demanding research. One was his garden, a lush almost tropical rain forest in Bloomington, which he tended dressed only in shorts, to the great scandal and outrage of his faculty neighbors. The other was his musicales, his playing of recorded masterworks, one of which I was once asked to attend.

I rather wished I hadn't. It was a solemn occasion. The major piece that Sunday evening was the Seventh Symphony of Sibelius—preceded by a short lecture on the talent and importance of the composer. We sat in a circle of chairs in absolute stillness. Then there were refreshments—an iced drink and some cookies—and the evening finished with some light harpsichording by Wanda Landowska and a few ripples on the harp by Zabaleta. I disgraced myself by upsetting my Kool-Aid (or whatever) on the carpet.

Kinsey delighted in trying small jests and tricks on me, whether to test me or just to amuse us both, I do not know. One sample will suffice.

By far the most sexually attractive person to me in the Kinsey entourage was Clyde Martin, the handsome young dark-haired statistician—happily married and unavailable. During one visit Kinsey fixed things so that Martin and I were left alone in the same room while Clyde changed his shirt, and gave me a good view of the polished marble of his arms and the well-defined plateau of his chest—while I looked and suffered and tapped my foot against the chair rung, a sure sign that a sexual thought was going through my head. But by then I was aware of Kinsey's sly and harmless trickery, so I made no suggestions to Clyde which I knew would be met with amused tolerance but flat refusal.

Kinsey later asked how things went.

"Oh, all right," I said, absorbed in studying a fingernail. "Nice of you to leave us alone—but too bad that I had seen my favorite policeman just that morning and was not in the mood for anything more at the moment."

Kinsey knew that my discontent with the academic matrix was growing. When I finally told him of my decision to quit the ivied nursery (the kindergarten that took care of the children until they were able to earn a living as adults) and become a tattoo artist, he reacted with the only critical statement I ever heard him make.

"Oh my God no," he said. "I've never interviewed anyone who didn't say he wanted his tattoo off."

But after a month or two his scientific curiosity began to assert itself. One day over dinner he said, "We really ought to take advantage of you."

"How so more than you already have?" I asked, sardonic.

"You are probably one of a half dozen literate tattoo artists in the country—if indeed that many. And we've noticed tattoos on hundreds of persons during the interviews. But they seem totally unable to tell us why they got them, and we don't have the time to probe as deeply as we would like."

"So . . . ?" I said.

"Keep a journal for us on the sexual motivations for getting tattoos," he said.

He liked the rambling investigations I kept for him, growing more interested as more details were discovered, and flattered me by saying I had unearthed information on tattooing which had never appeared in print before. He even suggested that we might collaborate on a monograph, but his early death in 1956 ended that project.

On several occasions Kinsey visited my shop, more or less incognito, spending five or six hours there on a busy Saturday. He talked to the swabbies and others, asking loaded questions that seemed entirely innocent. At the end of one such session he said: "I think every social worker or psychologist ought to spend at least five full days in field work in a tattoo shop before he gets his degree."

Towards the end of his life Kinsey changed. As sensitive as I was to semantics, having for years played with words in the classroom, I noticed first of all a change in his speaking habits. Before this, he had always used "we" and "us" when referring to the work and research of the Institute; and now it suddenly became "I" and "me." Puzzled, I said nothing—but there were other changes as well. He was now working so hard that the strain was telling on him and his heart; he kept flying back and forth to California, interviewing in all the prisons from San Quentin to Atascadero. And once when he came to visit my new apartment on a third floor, he came up the steps painfully and slowly. He paused at the last landing and looked up at me as I leaned over the banister.

"Oh Sam," he said, panting. "What have you done to me?"

But the changes were more pronounced than those in his pronouns. He began to illustrate what Gertrude Stein had said of Saroyan: "He cannot stand the weight of being great." Formerly, Kinsey would listen to you, nodding, agreeing, or raising objections. Now his statements became authoritative, almost ex cathedra pronouncements; he no longer listened quietly. Instead, he interrupted, issued dicta dogmatically, often turning impatient and snappish, sometimes arrogant, and even made cutting attacks on fellow scientists. Of course, at that time there were many serious pressures on him and the Institute, from political, financial, rightwing, and religious groups.

It was unfortunate, but one could really see the open and receptive mind closing down upon its grains of sand. To the end he did remain, however, an extraordinary man, an overwhelming personality. Had he been less zealous and devoted to his work than he was, he might have lived much longer. He was killed by overwork and his unwillingness to slow down. Instead of his flights to California he should have been resting.

105

But then, had he done so, had he controlled the demon within, he would not have been Doctor Kinsey.

If one really believed in an afterlife, it would be pleasant to consider Kinsey sitting with Socrates and Plato under the shade of an ilex tree discussing the *Phaedrus*, or asking Leonardo da Vinci about his golden youths, or Michelangelo about the models he used, or Whitman to tell the real truth about himself and Peter Doyle. Questioning and questing, he would have all eternity to roam in—and if he ever came to the end, he would still be unsatisfied.

Chapter VII

THE BIRTH OF PHIL ANDROS

I T MAY COME AS A SHOCK to some of the younger members of the homosexual community to realize that the freedom of expression obtainable in any adult bookstore (read "pornography") was not always there—that, as a matter of fact, such emporiums of lust and wickedness were opened only after 1966.

Before that time, what happened? We were all hunters, looking on every page for expressions that would be meaningful to us, relishing the hidden allusion, the double meaning. The college students of the 1920s delighted in the works of James Branch Cabell, who was for that generation what Tolkien was for the 1960s—except that Cabell was juicier, and when the candles went out and the fair ladies began to comment on the length of Jurgen's sword or his staff—or he to praise the lovely scabbards which they had—well, we all tittered and slyly underlined the passages, or made a page-reference note in the back of the book so that we could find the hotspot again.

There was some homosexual writing done in the 1920s and 30s, but it was a sad and sorry thing. A firm named Greenberg published much of that early stuff—mostly novels, all of which ended unhappily with the homosexual "hero" committing suicide or being killed in some way; thus sin was punished and middle-class virtue triumphed, and America could go happily blundering on its hypocritical puritan way.

Early in life I had dabbled in writing. *Pan and the Firebird*, the Cabellian sketches that I had done for Andrews' writing class, full of double-tenders and quite homosexual in tone, was published in 1930; only a Texas reviewer commented on the homosexuality and mentioned the "Libation to a Dead God" as being obviously about Valentino. *Angels on the Bough*, six years later, was a campus novel, winning the approbation of Gertrude Stein, Carl Van Vechten, and Thornton Wilder; it contained a heavily concealed homosexual character, but all the necessary hints to uncover him were there.

Gertrude, however, was right. "You can't write and teach, you know," she said fiercely, shaking me by the lapels. "The worst thing to do if you want to write is to teach and here's why. You teach all day and then that word-finding part of your brain is worn out and you can't find any words to put down on paper because that part of your brain is empty. It would be better yes much better to be a butcher."

Not only did I spend the next fifteen years teaching—and thus diminishing my urge to write—but for most of those years I was lost in the bottle, and no man can write while he's smashed. You can't even see the keys, let alone hit them.

When I abandoned university teaching for tattooing, and stopped drinking too, for ten years or more all was roses and beauty. The most handsome young men in the world came into the shop wanting tattoos—the blue-eyed Germans, the stalwart Poles, the dark and erotic Italians, the long-limbed Scandinavians—all lovely stereotypes, and lots of uglies too. My sex life discreetly flourished but my social life was ruined—long shop hours, few free evenings. And there was never any intellectual conversation; still, I listened to the customers and piled up a lot of stories.

Dimly through it all—the excitement, the crowds of young sailors on first "liberty"—but evermore receding was the dream of writing. True, in the long empty hours when no one came into the shop for servicing, I got a lot of reading done. Dr. Kinsey at one point gave me the name and address of *Der Kreis* (The Circle), a trilingual homosexual magazine published in Zurich, to which I subscribed. *One* magazine in the United States did not come into existence until 1952, thirty years after the inception of *Der Kreis*.

Through the 1930s and 40s *Der Kreis* was the only homosexual magazine generally available. It began as a small mimeographed four-sheet under the direction of a lesbian fondly known as Mamina who had founded the Swiss Friendship Bond in Switzerland. After several changes, Mamina handed the leadership over to Rolf, a well-known Swiss actor, and in 1943 the club became all-male, and the magazine was renamed *Der Kreis*. When I first knew the publication, it was a thin little thing of about thirty-six pages (more in some issues), the first half in German, the latter half divided between French and English, the English section added only in 1952. In each issue there were at least four pages of half-tone photographs—handsome young men, all discreetly covered, no frontal nudity allowed. And yet approximately every fourth issue of the magazine was withheld by U.S. Customs on the grounds that it was obscene—one of the most perverse and scandalous homophobic judgments ever made, solely on the ground the publication was homosexual.

And what stories they were, those little vignettes in *Der Kreis*! Sweet and sloppy, with lots of handholding and side-long glances and deep heartfelt sighs. Most had sad and sentimental endings; sometimes everything worked out all right, but the stories ended before anyone got into bed, or did much except sigh romantically and grin at each other. Yet in an effort to attract American subscribers, the work of a few notable Americans began to appear in the English section. Paul Cadmus sent photographs of his paintings and drawings, and George Platt Lynes sent his "non-profit-making ventures" as he called them—his excellently lighted, inventive, and beautiful photographs of extraordinarily handsome young men—at first allowing them to appear under his real name, and finally switching to the lens-name of Roberto Rolf. Of writers, James Barr (Fugate), author of *Quatrefoil* and *Derricks*, was the best-known American.

In 1958 the "English" editor—a roly-poly bilingual German living in Zurich—made his way to America to try to uncover new contributors and to introduce himself to those he had known only through correspondence. In Chicago he looked up a photographic studio which had sent him pictures, largely to advertise its name, as the

Athletic Model Guild on the west coast had done. Inevitably, returning from dinner one evening, I found this chubby little man sitting on my tattoo shop doorstep.

I must say that Rudolf Jung—or Burkhardt, as he sometimes called himself—was an expert in the spreading of honey. Flattery is a potent weapon, and he knew how to handle it perfectly. The result was that he teased me into composing—"at least an essay, if you don't feel like writing fiction"—for his magazine.

So began an alliance with *Der Kreis* which lasted until its demise in 1967. Rudolf drew me deeper and deeper into its workings, wheedling not only stories out of me but drawings as well, although I was never any good at those, and often asking me to help him rewrite some of his own things. Unfortunately, although he had a good critical mind, he could not produce fiction; it all sounded as if it had been written by Bret Harte, a narration *about* an event—no conversation or dialogue, an old-fashioned nineteenth-century technique of synopsis that read like a combination of Trollope and Dickens; the only thing lacking was the direct address to "Gentle Reader." There were no vivid sensory images, nothing to stimulate the imagination. "Help me rewrite this?" came more and more frequently from him—and in each case it meant recomposing the entire thing from beginning to end.

The era of pen names began, since there were never enough contributors. For *Der Kreis* I had several: "Donald Bishop" for sociological things such as "The Bull Market in America" (on hustling), and "Pussies in Boots" on the new leather movement. Some stories were written under "Ward Stames," a simple anagram of my real name. For poetry in the manner of Housman I became "John McAndrews." "Thomas Cave" produced more thoughtful and reflective stories, sometimes in the Thomas Mann manner. "Phil Andros" was not yet born.

Since I was going to Europe every Christmas to visit the ailing Alice Toklas, I managed to be present at quite a few of the Circle's New Year's Eve parties. Men danced together (horrors!) and held hands and kissed and drank champagne.

110

The orgy backroom had not yet been invented—but everyone seemed happy and content with the dancing.

All in all, however, it was rather a grim group that made up the leadership of the Circle. Most of the men were far along in years. Their attitudes were not keeping pace with the times, and those in control never found out or even wanted to find out how to bring young people into responsible positions. The Club and the magazine had lavishly supported a half-dozen old men, although the contributors never received a penny. When *Der Kreis* died in 1967, the reasons were given that as a movement it no longer had any purpose, the whole picture having been altered until there was no need for further reform. The truth was threefold: the leaders could not keep up with the very changes they had helped to bring about, there was a lack of money and subscribers, and Rolf went completely senile.

Eventually the confinements and restrictions of *Der Kreis* policies developed great feelings of claustrophobia in me. Anything explicitly or even tacitly sexual had to be removed because of the danger of being charged with prurience or obscenity. The handholdings and sighs and glances came to seem utterly unreal in a world where people sucked and fucked.

I had rather delicately expressed such feelings to Rudolf from time to time. Now I was firmer.

"This is the gah-damnedest crap I ever laid eyes on," I said, shaking a recent issue under his nose.

"Ah yes," he said. "I felt you were growing a little restless."

"I wanna write about real life," I said.

"Well," said Rudolf, "there's Kim Kent in Copenhagen. He's got two magazines—*eos* and *amigo*—in Danish, German, and English. Why don't you send him something? I haven't told you about him because I don't want to lose you. If I give you his address, will you still write for us?"

"Yeah, yeah," I said. And so I sent Kim Kent a story called "The Sergeant with the Rose Tattoo," which he entered in a short story contest he was having at the moment, and it won a fifty dollar first prize. Big deal. Kim was as adept at flattery as Rudolf was—the sure mark of an editor who wants contributors for nothing.

Meanwhile, back at the raunch in Chicago, in 1962 tattooing was about to be closed down. Well, not closed entirely—but the age limit for it was being raised to twenty-one. This was happening at the same time that the penalties for homosexual encounters were being lifted in Illinois, and the "age of consent" for male-male sex lowered to eighteen, all this through the singlehanded efforts of Kinsey. Tattoo buffs commented about the law raising the tattoo age limit to twenty-one—which automatically cut out all the boot sailors from Great Lakes; they felt that the mark on the psyche of an early homosexual experience might be more damaging than an anchor tattooed on the arm. I avoided the argument, but I sensed the closing of the doors and began to think of doing other things.

The owner of the photo studio whom I had known since Rudolf's visit in 1958—a matter of five years—was in the shop one day. We had always had a very amicable arrangement. Since I had to be discreet about whom I propositioned, I would send him the beauties whom he would photograph in a posing strap, selling the pictures to his considerable nation-wide clientele. In turn he would send me handsome hustlers who were not reluctant to earn a few bucks to buy eggs and oysters.

To this guy, then, I was idly turning over in conversation various flaky possibilities about what I might do when I closed my shop at the end of 1962.

"I might move the tattoodling business to Paris," I said, remembering that in my first story for Kim Kent I had already done so. "Or to San Francisco. Or I might go back to writing," I added wistfully.

"Nuts," said he. "You're too fuckin' old to write."

Well!

I was galvanized. Spurred to action. Nothing that anyone could have said would have sent me more quickly to a typewriter. Forgotten were the years of listening to my internal critic who had been whispering daily that I was burned out, that I had nothing more to say, that everything had been said

112

already. And to hell with even the question of money—I'd write just to please myself, and Kim Kent and Rudolf, and (as I have said a thousand times) lonely old men whacking off in hotel rooms at night. It is amazing how a chance remark, forgotten by the maker, can move one to violent and long-lasting activity.

I'd had a lot of experience with hustlers, I'd read John Rechy's *City of Night*. It was a stunning book for those years, but at the same time Rechy's waffling attitude about his nameless hustler was annoying; I had the feeling he was holding back, afraid to reveal himself, carefully cultivating the icy center of his being and saving it for—what or whom? I didn't know.

I had always liked the name "Phil," having chosen it for my tattoo-name along with the "Sparrow" borrowed from Skelton's poem. And as one who had once taught semantics, it was easy to return the word "philander"—grossly altered from its original meaning in a heterosexual matrix—to its pristine form: "philos"—to love, and "andros" man—thus Phil Andros might be taken either as "lover-man" or "man-lover." In a sense my friend the pimp had been midwife to the birthing of Phil Andros.

The tattoo shop was closed, and with Cliff Raven—whom I had helped to start in tattooing—I went to Milwaukee on weekends, where the age limit for swabbies was still eighteen. Every Friday afternoon I boarded the old North Shore electric, bearing a tablet of yellow legal paper, and began to write. The hour's trip gave me a good start on a Phil Andros story—all tailored for Kim Kent. For most of 1963–64 I sent him a story each month, and occasionally still sent one to Rudolf. Once I even sent one to *Der Kreis* under the name of Phil Andros. Old Rolf, the chief editor, nearly had apoplexy: "I will not have that beast's name appearing in our pages!" was his gentle way of rejecting me.

Very early I considered the different ways of telling a story, and decided—for verisimilitude—to narrate them in the first person. Thus Edgar Allan Poe, according to the best critical analyses, gained belief more easily for his stories by using "I." And to that technique I added the "eponymous"—of having the narrator-hustler's name of Andros appear also as that of author.

The method seemed to work. I stumbled around with two or three inconsequential stories at first—and then finally with one hit on what was evidently an archetypal theme: how a white guy (not Phil) submitted himself as a slave to a black, in order to atone for all the past sins of whites against blacks.

Sometimes Kim Kent got five or six letters a month commenting about his stories or his magazine. Imagine his surprise when "The Blacks and Mr. Bennett" brought him over a hundred letters! Phil Andros was thus "established," and the readers clamored for a sequel, and I went on writing.

I wanted Phil to be as honest with himself as he was with his clients, and to progress and develop. In the earlier stories he was not sure of his own sexual identity, only gradually becoming completely homosexual. He was the anti-hero turned hero by a curious twisting of fate—his Greek good looks joined to an educated brain in a macho body, the whole overlaid with an ability to empathize and feel compassion. And so he began his wanderings, like those of Ulysses, through a world peopled with a diversity of "clients"—bank presidents, young gangsters, college boys and professors, weightlifters and policemen, fetishists and motorcyclists, millionaires and narcissists, factory workers and interior decorators—something for everyone. I tried to give Phil an advantage over most hustlers I had known—to make him observant and literate, able to relate what he saw with wryness and sometimes venom, with an unconcealed pleasure in the things belonging to passion, and gentleness for things of the intelligence and the spirit. More than three-fourths of Phil's adventures had a basis in fact—out of my own experience or that of acquaintances.

The success of Phil Andros in the Danish magazines was astonishing. He was called the "American Jean Genet"—although that *certainly* was wrong! He was complimented in letters for a kind of writing that was new and different in plot and style, far removed from the well-worn patterns of the unhappy homosexual novels of the 1930s and 40s, before the Great Explosion of pornography.

Despite the comparative freedom of expression allowed in the Danish magazines, the early Andros stories were not hardcore. Nearly every one was preceded by a cautionary note from Kim Kent: " . . . warn our more sensitive readers against reading this story" . . ."For grown-up readers only" . . ."our firm belief in our readers' maturity the only justification for having printed this" . . ."no pleasant children's tale" . . . and so forth. The stories weren't really all that extreme, but Kim Kent was protecting himself against possible repercussions even though Denmark had relaxed its antiporn laws almost to the vanishing point. Phil had a great deal more freedom than in *Der Kreis*, yet there was no use of four-letter words.

In the United States in the mid-1960s a case came before the Supreme Court, one intended to settle the question of obscenity, the famous Roth decision, in which the nine quarrelsome old men came to the conclusion that obscenity had three criteria: 1) it had to appeal to the prurient interest of the average man; 2) it had to violate contemporary community standards; and 3) it had to be utterly without any redeeming social value.

Whammo! There was a thoughtful pause whilst the country digested that, and came to the conclusion that the community meant the country as a whole, and that of course there was a revelatory and redeeming social value to even the lousiest suckee-fuckee books.

The gates were opened. The flood began. Suddenly *all* the old four-letter words (and some new ones) appeared in print, almost overnight. Publishers no longer had to write prefatory notes condemning what they were printing; they could merely suggest the social significance of erotica, and lo! all was satisfied. The court's decision had more holes in it than a colander, and publishing houses sprang up like mushrooms after rain.

One of the older homosexual presses which had been weaseling its way carefully between the markers was the Guild Press, presided over by a jolly rotundity who had been in trouble with the law before, and had even voluntarily committed himself (it was alleged) to the mental ward at St. Elizabeth's Hospital—whence he ran his press with the insouciance that Leigh Hunt had shown a century and a half before, when he continued his literary works while in prison.

A New York bookseller put me in touch with this jolly Roger, suggesting that if he wanted to upgrade the reputation of his press with some softcore hard-cover homosexual literature, he ought to consider adding Andros to his list.

And so *$tud* was born—eighteen connected stories from *eos* and *amigo* gathered together and called a novel. A contract was signed over a pittance, galleys were read in 1966, and Phil—now in California—waited breathlessly for his book to appear.

It didn't. Dead silence from the Jolly Roger in Washington, D.C. No response to a dozen letters, the runaround on phone calls. Three years went by. Phil later learned that the J.R. had run out of money and couldn't pay the binder.

There were many confusions over the book. J. Brian in San Francisco brought out a paperback edition; then the hard-cover edition was remaindered as soon as it appeared, and a sleazy three-volume paperback set with dreadful pictures was produced by the Jolly Roger's press, without Phil's name anywhere to be seen.

Naturally, that was the end of any dealings with J.R. To amuse myself, I turned to the production of some novels, slightly harder core than the Danish stories. Frenchy's *Parisian Press* in San Francisco published *My Brother the Hustler, San Francisco Hustler, When in Rome, Do . . .* and *The Joy Spot*, all in the early 1970s. Kim Kent in Copenhagen published a handsome trilingual edition of *The Joy Spot* under the title *Ring Around the Rosy*. The porn market being what it was, Phil was not surprised to see a pirating of *San Francisco Hustler* (with "Biff Thomas" billed as the author) under the title of *Gay in San Francisco*. Only the characters' names were changed—to protect the thieves.

Finally the Nine Old Men of the Supreme Court decided to take another whack at obscenity, not satisfied with the tumult and the shouting that their first decision had caused. This time they added a few nasties: they said that "community

116

standards" could be those of any or all communities—cities, towns, villages, hamlets, states, localities, or counties. Thus San Francisco's liberal standards might allow unlimited circulation of porn, but what about Peoria or Des Moines? What's exciting and pleasurable in one place may be anathema and apoplexy-inducing in another. Furthermore, "to redeeming social value" they added "literary and artistic." Confusion—devastating and complete. Alexander Pope's couplet describes it best:

> Thy hand, Great Anarch, lets the curtain fall,
> And universal darkness buries all.

A firm called Greenleaf had published Phil's *Renegade Hustler* just before the second decision, but its quasi-sequel—*The Greek Way*—was delayed for three years after the Court had had its second say.

In Denmark ten years after the laws regarding pornography were canceled, more than half of the purveyors and publishers had gone out of business for lack of money. The same thing has happened in the United States. All novelty has worn off, and the sales of porn have dropped considerably. This is not to say that there is no market for it, but only that the interest has diminished. In "adult" bookstores you will still find the aisles crowded with voyeur-readers with hardons, leafing through the magazines which have not been sealed in cellophane.

One of the reasons for the decline is the publisher's insistence that a certain "percentage of pages" (at least fifty percent) be devoted to sexual scenes graphically described. Another reason is the language used. Everyone knows the technique of the sob sister in journalism or on TV, who with crude accounts seeks to get effects by setting up a superficial excitement with highly colored description. In the same way, the ordinary porn-writer attempts to affect his readers by using lots of four-letter words, thus cutting away all chance for the imagination to be deeply activated and to build up its greater powers. He does not give the reader a map to direct his fantasies, but hauls him instead into a rubberneck sightseeing bus—and shouts to him through a megaphone what to look at and what to feel about it. The man who says "motherfucker" every third word soon becomes drearily ineffective, but the bishop who inserts a "damn" into a sentence is not quickly forgotten.

How then to write porn in the most effective way? Phil Andros can give no lessons, but merely say that he has always approached a scene slowly, never plunging into the action too fast; that he has attempted to use vivid and sensory images from all the senses, thereby drawing the reader along with him into the sexual encounter; that he has always trusted the accumulation of details, knowing that each one plucks at a harpstring somewhere inside a person, and that those stimuli compel the imagination to emerge slowly—tremblingly alive—causing the corpus cavernosum to be gradually inflated and pumped full of blood. Then—if Phil has taken his own advice and been diligent—perhaps the ultimate reward will follow: the sudden involuntary clutch of the vesicle muscles around their contents, the convulsive shudder, the thrusting spurt through the urethra, and the deposit of literally billions of tiny invisible tadpole-things upon the silken ribbing of the pouch of one's athletic supporter.

And the porn-writer's version of such a sentence? "He came in his pants" or "he creamed his jeans."

Chapter VIII

FAREWELL, MY LOVELIES

W HEN I LEFT CHICAGO FOR California, I found the
roots that had to be pulled up had gone very deep.
It was not possible to leave the lovely dirty old city without
taking note of some of the bodies I remembered best of all.
Each of them answered some demand of my being or one of
my different selves.

As the years went on I passed into the land where Everyman must eventually go, that of the older human being.
The carefree life of one's prime, and the ease with which
romantic encounters had been so carelessly and happily
made—those things vanished so slowly that one was
scarcely aware they were diminishing. But go they did,
leaving a kind of bittersweet afterglow, a flickering tapes-
try of golden memories, from which now and again one
arose with nostalgia and a barren pleasure.

No question: one had to begin to purchase, or do
without—and here again in Chicago the studio which had
pimped for me helped enormously. They sent me many
young men who answered my needs, and the affection that
developed in me for a few of them rounded out the picture
of my desires—from sleek and compact Latin to blond and
stalwart Nordic. Each of them fulfilled a fantasy of mine,
and I am grateful to them all.

There was Guido—a dark and brooding Italian with the
sullen moods and romantic charm of a Latin Heathcliff, and
no thundercloud shot of the young Olivier against the
storm-sky of *Wuthering Heights* ever surpassed Guido in
beauty and passion. At twenty years of age he was still
engaged in the perfection of his small body; he exercised
and lifted weights, and his small frame carried a classic
musculature which I had seldom encountered before.

I came as close to falling for him completely (in limerence, to use the new term for lovesickness) as I had ever done with anyone, and for somewhat over four years saw him at least once a week and sometimes more. When it came to a tally of the money spent on him—down payments on cars, reduction of debts—I was startled. Yet why not? The money was flowing into the tattoo shop in a golden stream, and it might as well have been spent on Guido as on anything or anyone else.

In a story about Guido, "Jungle Cat," I said what I had always believed—that the body of a man was the most beautiful creation in the world; and that every sculptor since the beginning had praised it above the female form. And Guido's body was perfect. In movement or repose it was as flawless as a Chinese poem, a sonnet by Keats, a concerto by Mozart. When he was active, moving his arms or legs, his muscles flickered into excited life. To see him pick up a book, and watch the counterpoint of his muscles turning against each other was like listening to a harp arpeggio; to see him bend to tie a shoelace was better than Beethoven. In repose, with a forearm flung across his eyes, the side muscles running above his ribs looked like the two hands of a jealous lover clutching him from behind; and the black curls of his armpits were more entrancing than the head of Medusa. His long slim brown fingers repeated in miniature the beauty of his body, exquisite as a carving in topaz . . . His feet were high-arched and perfect, his skin clear and unblemished and tawny with the residue of the Mediterranean sun. The eyelashes hardly belonged to a man's face; they were long and black, and beneath them intense dark eyes looked out. The eyebrows grew in a straight black line clear across the bridge of his nose, dipping slightly downward in the middle—calm, but with mobility in them. At moments one end would shoot upwards like a startled bird from cover, extraordinarily expressive. Guido was all youth and firmness and silk, and he turned the shabby old backroom of my shop into a place where we were alone on the isles beneath the wind, with the warm dark night around us and the ice-cold moon above.

Yah—facile, romantic! I was never in love, perhaps because I preferred a multifold experience rather than a long commitment to a single idealized love-object. But I came close to the edge of danger with Guido ... Had I the capacity for love, or was I intended to be a solitary with such poverty of spirit that I could never enlarge myself to take in another? Was I too much an egoist? The most dangerous of all egoists is the one skilled in what seems to be self-effacement, one whose outer kindness and gentleness really mask a complete and total centering on self, with a thorough indifference to others.

So—Guido nearly tore down the granite wall. John Donne said, in a well-known passage from which Hemingway chose a title, that no man was an island, entire in himself; that we are all a part of the whole, and that no one should ever send to ask for whom the bell tolls since "it tolls for thee."

This is all wrong. It is obvious today that each man *is* an island, eternally sealed away from his fellows, whose mind-workings—even the simplest—he can never know. And no matter how much in love, in limerence, Everyman remains isolated and alone. Let us change, then, the last part of Donne's quotation to: "And therefore, baby, don't bother to send to learn for whom the bell tolls; as long as thou canst *hear* it ringing, you'll know it's *not* for thee."

And perhaps my ghetto wall crumbled a little more with Friedrich—Guido's extreme opposite. Here was the great-thewed bridegroom—blond, Nordic, Austrian, blue-eyed, a weightlifter and once a Mr. Illinois, perhaps the single most photographed "model" of the 1950s and 60s. Seeing him, one would hardly think he was a male prostitute, a hustler—tall, with corn-silk hair and innocence on his forehead. His chest was tremendous, bulging—to think of it limited and contained by the frail fabric of a white cotton T-shirt gave you a feeling of unreality. His upper arms were as brawny as those of Hercules; he was bursting with health and blond godliness. In summer his tan was red-gold deep, and the charm of his body's radiance as blinding as an electric arc. In the gym he frequented, all the small types veered towards him as if he were the true magnetic north, but he avoided them all. What seemed to be arrogance and stiffness in his nature was really shyness, perhaps a basic insecurity, for he was not very well educated. But he had the disease of beauty, which in its progression rots the soul and destroys the will. Something happens to innocence when—as you walk unclothed on the beach, or clothed on the street—you know that every third person, male or female, would like to go to bed with you.

It was not unreasonable to assume that occasionally Apollo or Hercules, tiring of love on Olympus, would now and then come to earth again and momentarily assume a human form, to make love to us poor mortals. And having sex with a god is quite a jolt to one's universe; it takes some little time thereafter for the nebulae to stop their spiral whirling, and for the stars to settle back into their familiar and accustomed constellations.

This young god (masquerading this time as a send-over from the pimping service) had arisen from my bed—and as my sight gradually returned I watched him standing in front of my full-length mirror, idly flexing his great muscles, treating me to a view of the tanned and incredible landscape of his back, his torso, those great-columned legs lighted with the soft luminance of the golden hair that covered them. I watched the poetry of his movements as muscle answered muscle, springing into indolent or rapid life as he ordered his body to do his bidding. His profile was godlike as he tilted his chin upwards, and godlike the full face front as his eyes, half-smiling, looked at me from under the sweep of his golden hair, bleached by the summer sun until the end-points seemed tipped with silver. His massive tawny shoulders tapered down the wonderful terrain of his torso to the slender waist, ending in the smoky gold of the softly curling hair . . .

So he posed and moved, and posed again. How had it happened that he should have liked and trusted me? True, I had put forth a great effort to understand him. I talked to him only about himself and his golden-brown body, and arranged mirrors so that he could see himself in action (for I knew there were no mirrors on Olympus—and moreover, I quickly recognized his narcissism), and was generous with his fees. And while he posed I pulled forth from the caverns of my mind the symphonies he did not hear, and read the poems he could not see. Then I thought of the right thing, the best comparison to make (although I had said it before to others and had only half meant it) and I said:

"You remind me of some young god who has just stepped down from the frieze on the Parthenon."

The blue eyes, and the blank blank look—as the synapses failed once again to connect. "Whatdyuhmean—the freeze on the parking lot?"

Ah well, there, Freddie (more "American," he thought, than Friedrich), who cares about the Parthenon or the parking lot? After I left for California he became a Chicago cop, I heard, and in moments of musing I wondered just how he managed to handle the scene, where daily he might have met or been recognized by his previous "scores." Would he scowl and pass by, swinging his nightstick, never acknowledging a murmured greeting of any kind? Or would he have sought out his former clients and perhaps suggested a bit of blackmail, despite the "legality" of things in Illinois? What did the police chief say about all those poses of his in tiny cache-sexes, those profiled bulges behind wet thin cloth? or did he know? And what did Friedrich's erstwhile scores say of him? Perhaps they blackmailed *him*, thus feathering their caps by saying they had had a cop in full uniform.

And moving on . . . there was thirty-two-year-old Roy Robinson, toothless, a bum, a hanger-on in the tattoo shop, con man, thief (he burglarized my place three times, and was always stealing whatever he could make away with to pawn). But he had a very skilled and useful mouth and furnished me with an extraordinary sensation—for a price, although I never touched him sexually. Roy was continually having wife trouble of one sort or another; whether she knew of the services his toothless gums performed for several, I never learned. But one chilly autumn night in Chicago he jumped into the cold water of Lake Michigan, and that was the end of Roy—as mixed-up a person as I had ever known, and perhaps the most dishonest, truly afflicted with anomie—no moral sense, no obligations, no loyalties; one who, as a current saying had it, would have sold the blood in his mother's veins for a buck. Yet there was something that made you like him while you pitied him—and he was helpful in many ways around the shop, cleaning and sweeping and mopping. But in ten years of knowing him I was never able to trust him.

And farewell, too, to my skinny aesthetic friend, Reggie, who hated his last name so much because of its easy confusion with that of John Dillinger (shot by the FBI outside the Biograph Theatre in Chicago) that he dropped it and used his middle name thereafter. Reggie was a ballet dancer, not a very good one—but acting on my advice he began to study Labanotation very early in the game, and became an authority on it. If you needed oral gratification, Reggie had just what was satisfying to work on, being excessively equipped; but having pleasured himself he could never bring happiness to his partner, which led to our eventual parting. Reggie was exceedingly effeminate, but sometimes one could put up with swish if Nellie had something everyone wanted. And Reggie did.

Wandering in these pleasant forests and preserves of a highly selective memory brings me to a trio—for you could not know one without knowing all. But the one I knew especially was Larry, who had two identical-triplet brothers, Louie and Lester. In 1963 they were all eighteen, and that was the year that Larry—hearing from a benchmate in the factory where he worked that I had to do with hustlers—got my name and address. And so one evening a gawky six-foot-two adolescent came to see me, knowing nothing about anything. When he left, putting on his windbreaker, there dropped to the floor a lightweight imitation meat cleaver about four inches long with handle, weighing perhaps three ounces. I burst out laughing.

"To protect yourself?" I finally managed, and he nodded and escaped.

I still know Larry, now in his mid-thirties, and Louie and

Lester too; they were all three naked one night in my apartment, to my great confusion; and they all had a thin white line across their bellies where they had been cramped together before birth—or as Larry explained it: "There wasn't womb for all three." The father vanished on seeing the trio pop out, and the mother in great dismay consigned them for highschool to Boys' Town, from which they escaped twenty times in two years. Curiously, each of them was a kind of drifter; Larry himself in fifteen years held over forty jobs, and had been married three times, with one shackup. Louis was similarly rootless and twice divorced, and Lester was homosexual, which should say enough about his general qualities of permanence and fidelity. Thus Larry was bi, Louie hetero, and Lester homo, a curious division; and as the old wives might have it, perhaps they shared one soul among three. Their sibling rivalry was intense, and they claimed to get "flashes" of intuitive knowledge from each other, no matter how widely separated. But they were really identical, except Larry's bent to the left, Louie's to the right, and Lester's straight down. Or up. And it was Louis who in a phone call many years later said to me: "You seem to be a focal point around which so many lives revolve. Ours, too. You'll always be there."

Hah!

Then there was Bob Berbich, whom I cruised in a bar at the end of World War II; he was in a sailor's uniform, and both of us were drunk. "I'd like to go witcha," he said, "but I'm broke."

Magnanimity! "Oh, thass all right," I said loftily. "This time's on the house, account you is one of our boys in blue."

He learned soon enough that all was free in my place, and so he began to take advantage of it—and our knowing each other went on for innumerable times. Sixteen years after our first meeting he reciprocated. But in all those years Bob really answered several of my needs; he was successively a sailor, a motorcycle delivery messenger, a taxi driver, a night steelworker, and a uniformed guard. In my growing preference for the blue collar instead of the white, these occupations were just what I needed for my fantasies.

125

And just possibly for his too. He was not very bright, and his language was "dese" and "dose." But he loved the glory-hole I put into the door of the head in my tattoo shop and made good use of it. What odd little imaginings passed through his brain, his three pounds of dimly conscious meat as he stood facing the plywood two inches from his nose, I'll never know—nor, I guess, would I be very much interested.

Then there was a Mom-infested person with a grave and horrid stammer, a tall lean handsome guy with a good face and a growing fascination with psychic masochism. His name was Tom, and he was the one who owned both a motorcycle and a concert-size harp, who combined narcissism and exhibitionism within himself. On him I put five large tattoos—an eagle on the chest, panthers and daggers and dragons and such like on his arms; and helped him cut the silver cord which bound him to Mommy, whereupon his stammer largely vanished. He was a grand person and extremely good-looking; I regret that my demand for the real thing in a sexual encounter—not the sort of play-pretend activity he enjoyed—so extinguished his desire and upset him that he fled back home from California and was not heard from after that.

There was also a remarkable hustler whose nickname was "Cherokee." In those days he was considered the best. He was perhaps the most professional hustler I had ever known—with perfect bedroom manners, cooperative, unshockable, and with an intuition which never failed him; he always seemed to know exactly what to do to bring comfort and surcease from pain to his clients—and quite possibly his good reputation rested on that. If towards the end of his career he began somewhat to run to fat, he nonetheless maintained his list because of his manners, and because his clients were sentimentally attached to him. He extended his hustling career until he was well into his late thirties—and perhaps for all I know he may even yet be occasionally selling himself in the vasty desert of the Midwest where he lived.

And finally, my cops.

The first was a guy whom I had possibly met in the Lincoln

Baths before I stopped drinking. I do not know how he got my name and telephone number; perhaps I gave them to him while I was drunk, perhaps someone else passed them to him. I remember that the circumstances of our getting together were rather mysterious—a phone call or two, and then a visit. He gave me the name of "Bob McDonald" but I did not think it was the right one. Since I was cautious, after our first romantic encounter I looked into his wallet while he went to the bathroom, to see if McDonald were his real name. Imagine the shock when the wallet opened on a Chicago police badge, number 4468. He came back from his ablutions, and it took all of my histrionic abilities, developed in twenty years in the classroom, to keep my voice steady, to be polite, to say yes, I would like to see him again. When he left I collapsed trembling into a chair.

I need not have worried overmuch. He reciprocated in every possible way—and we knew each other for six or seven years. He never revealed his job, and I rather enjoyed the "status" that having a cop gave me. In 1956 I got a sad phone call from him. He had been in an accident and a leg had to be amputated; in a heavy depression he announced his departure for California, and I never heard from him again.

The second cop was a tall handsome young man, rather slender, for whom every attractive police uniform in the world seemed to have been designed. He was on the Milwaukee police force for a time, and his name was Jim; I tattooed him in Milwaukee and furnished him with gin as he walked his downtown beat. The Milwaukee winter uniform was sexually very attractive to me—the dark blue coat had a double row of brass buttons rising to curve outwards towards the shoulders, and a high tight collar to enclose the neck. He was completely hetero—but even so, at that time something was askew in his head, for he confessed to me that with women—and also when masturbating, he could rarely develop an erection. That uniform of his which he wore so jauntily, with the cap pulled so low that the bridge almost covered his eyes, made me foolish enough to spend a considerable amount on Jim-baby; and although his problem was the same with me as with his women, it did not keep him from orgasm and enjoyment.

The third cop was a tattoo buff—or at any rate one who enjoyed the feel of the needle. I tattooed him in the shop (and made him the protagonist of a story by Phil Andros). His name was John, and for all I know he may still be on the Chicago police force. After carefully quizzing him to see that he completely understood the then-new Illinois law regarding homosexual encounters, I asked him if he considered the tattoo shop a "private place."

"If the door were locked, and you went into the backroom behind the curtain," he said.

I locked the door and we went into the backroom behind the curtain. Afterwards he asked if he could see me again, and delighted, I said yes.

"I was just wondering if sometime you would mind showing up in uniform," I said, for he had been in plainclothes (with his gun) when he came into the shop.

"Does that make it better?" he asked.

"N-no, not n-necessarily," I stammered, trapped in an unanswerable question.

"It sort of adds the frosting on the cake, huh?" he said, twinkling a bit.

"Exactly."

And that was the way he showed up from then on. I liked Johnny; he was a wild one—and since there was no way to get in touch with him (discretion for his job with the fuzz!) I had to leave Chicago without giving him my address in California.

The fondness I had for the police was an indication, I suppose, of the deeply buried residue of guilt from my childhood which accounted for my psychic masochism. One can never get entirely rid of those doleful shreds and tatters of the early impressments—in my case, the stern and austere puritanism of my Methodist maiden aunts and my narrow upbringing. And the policeman—well, he was the single point at which the law touched the individual, the ultimate authority—and when he was young and handsome, he could hold me in his hands and shape me like clay. If cops could only realize how deeply attracted many of us are to them, they would never have to go horny again. If they were in uniform—and perhaps only then—they could find comfort on any park bench, or in the shadows of any alley, or in the warmth of many expensive apartments. But the uniform would have to be in sight or be worn—cap, gunbelt, and boots at least. Without the symbols of power, a naked cop would be just another naked body.

There were others in my life—even some with whom for a while I shared myself and opened my mind and heart. The "Stud File" is full of cards and names and bits of coded information. The glass jar is packed with snippets of crinkly hair taken from my favorite persons, for when I was seventeen I knew I was going to be seventy. And there were going to have to be tangibles to which the imagination and memory could be tied, devices to stimulate nostalgia and the remembrance of things past. I was getting ready for the days when the "island-spirit" would be truly alone—without youth to visit me or to be ensnared, when the sort of happiness which Sophocles described might descend—the ultimate freedom from the "mad master" of sexual desire.

Chapter IX

A BONSAI TREE, A DOG OR TWO, AND AN OKTOBERFEST

S EVERAL HOLIDAY SEASONS AGO, my sister Virginia asked me to go with her to pick out a Christmas present.

"But shouldn't it be a surprise?" I asked.

"You have to pick out the one you want."

She took me to a nursery where they had a large collection of bonsai trees. I almost covered my face with my hands in horror.

"Please, no . . . no," I said.

"Why ever not?" she asked.

I was ashamed. "I simply can't be responsible for any living thing," I said. "It's just too much."

She was stunned, and later teased me about it.

Yet something else happened. My landlady's ancient father died, and Eva's daughter got her a long-haired dachshund for company, a feisty little beast named Fritz. And then Eva died. The front house was rented for one year, and then two, by two separate young married couples, both marriages breaking up. The dog was rented with the house, like a fixture. But in the third year, the renters were a couple with a large Doberman—and Fritz was homeless. I had enjoyed his company for four years, his scratching at my door every morning, without having any of the responsibility—but now he was forced on me. Either I had to take him or give him away.

I could not part with him, and reluctantly assumed responsibility. For the first few weeks I kept asking all my acquaintances if they didn't want a dog—and then gradually it all changed. I fell in love with him, I was smitten, I was lovesick, I was in limerence. I began to adore every

130

hair on his bullnecked, broad-chested, bandy-legged black and tan body. I taught him tricks, and was amazed at his vocabulary of a hundred and twenty words and phrases.

The sudden upspring of love and affection for the friendly little beast astounded me. It was as if all my life I had been waiting for an object on which to pour out all the accumulated love I had been storing up for so many years. At first it was somewhat frightening, and then I succumbed completely—walking him four or five times a day (good for me too), and adjusting my life to take care of him. And so I saw him through an attack by one of the savage free-running dogs from the commune a few doors away, and through various back ailments, which many long-spined dachshunds have. But alas, I could do nothing when—wagging his tail and his rear end in his great enthusiasm over a visitor—he ruptured his spine. Then followed an expensive operation, which did not work. He had to be destroyed.

For a full month I was beset with sudden furious shattering tear-storms, more intense and agonizing than anything I had ever felt for the death of a member of my human family. I shed more tears for Fritz than for my father, whose death had left me dry-eyed. And then I decided that I had to find another dog.

It was a search that ended at a kennel in Novato, where a small beastie had been kept for sixteen months, and was scheduled for destruction because his breeder felt that his front paws turned out too much for him to succeed as a show dog or a sire. I found his stance rather charming; it reminded me of the ballet fifth position. He looked exactly like Fritz— *pointes de feu*, fire-points above his eyes, tan "gloves" and all. But he lacked most of a dog's instincts because he had not had enough human love and contact during the formative weeks. He could not fetch or play ball; he could not dig (being raised on concrete) nor did he recognize a bird. After a while I found him a companion, an identical puppy (actually his great nephew), and he came to life. Number one was Blackstone; number two was Cranford—and Blackstone turned out to be completely homosexual. Every morning Blackstone licked Cranford, who like any piece of rough

131

trade casually chewed on a bone whilst being serviced.

Yet who cared? Every night I switched off the telephone, and to remind myself to turn it on in the morning, dropped a plastic rose on the carpet. One morning Blackie picked up the stem between his teeth, and like a shaggy Carmen sat up on his hindquarters and pawed at me with his front feet. So the three of us, fretted by life but still enjoying its pleasures, settled down to living together.

Berkeley by the 1970s had cooled off considerably after the riotous tumults of the 1960s. I adjusted rather rapidly to the loss of my "authority" which I had enjoyed in the tattoo shop—where I was absolute boss; if I didn't want to work on a person who was drunk or obnoxious or offensive I would tell him to get the hell out, using the "tone of authority" which the classroom years had developed. Nonetheless, I could understand why so many executives of corporations, or those in authority, crumpled and declined and even died when their power was diminished.

The drug culture in Berkeley had begun to settle down to the relatively harmless use of pot—which only insidiously and slowly weakened the will and the urge-to-work of its heaviest users. Heroin had been discouraged among the university students. And the fashion of LSD had passed— the great drug of hope, the mind-expanding magic that would turn everyone into Einstein, Mozart or Leonardo, that would make Everyman a genius. Nothing had turned out the way it had been predicted. The hallucinogens helped its takers to produce rock noise, psychedelic posters in fluorescent inks, artsy-craftsy belt buckles, puka-shell necklaces, copper bracelets, zodiac pendants, elaborate roach-holders and joint clips—all the eternal and enduring kitsch of the half-talented and ignorant who (knowing nothing of the past) had to reinvent for themselves even such symbols as yin and yang. In Berkeley there were spawned and flourished the rock groups with weird names and mayfly lives, playing at tiny clubs to ears no longer functional; here too were the little presses, publishing the arcane incomprehensible nonsense of young "poets" talking to themselves in public. The sidewalks of Telegraph

Avenue were lined with street merchants displaying their crudely fashioned wares on blankets. And the long straggly hair, the full beards and mustaches, persisted in many pockets and communes long after it had become old-fashioned everywhere else. Unwashed clones still quoted Chairman Mao long after he had fallen into disfavor and been abandoned even in China. If you wanted to see the scruffy barrel-bottom scrapings of the 1960s, you should come to the Land That Time Forgot—Berkeley.

I neither approved nor disapproved of all this; I merely observed, with whatever detachment I could summon. And I was certainly not without my own sins. In *The Magic Mountain* Thomas Mann describes how the inhabitants of the tuberculosis sanitarium at Davos in Switzerland passed from one amusement, one consuming fad or fashion or diversion to another—from amateur photography to stamp collecting, or any of a dozen other pastimes. All these things Mann described with one phrase that lingered permanently in my memory: "sinking back into the great dullness."

Until my reason reasserted itself, and the long years of preparation for these do-nothing days could be put into effect—I fell victim to Mann's disease. With me it took the form of collecting clocks, all the kinds and types I could afford, until my house had thirty-one of them, striking synchronously on Sundays when they were wound and reset, and drawing gradually apart as the week progressed and the springs unwound. Who can say to what extent this interest in watching the visible passing of time had been influenced by my early reading of the excursion on the subject of Time in Mann's masterwork.

Another example of the mindless "sinking into the great dullness" took hold of me: I built electronic gadgets and instruments from kits and instruction books—a color TV, a stereo music center, digital clocks, intrusion alarms, even doorbells that could be programmed to play tunes (I chose "Gaudeamus igitur" for its melancholy view of youth).

Thus my life arranged itself—and Phil Andros springing full-grown from my temple, like Athena from the brow of Zeus, was a pleasant surprise, helping me to pass the time;

in him and through him for several years I relived the adventures not only of my own youth but those of several others I had known.

And there were friends—some young, some old, and new ones made. Two of them each year celebrated with an Oktoberfest, a gathering of middle-aged queens (and a few young ones) who came to drink, eat brownies heavy with marijuana, and gossip. Each year I vowed I would never go again—and each year I went. Don drove me—a friend since my earliest days in Berkeley, who had chauffered me everywhere—a big man and very strong, excellent at opening cans. To my griping he paid no attention, reminding me that I complained about going every year.

"I don't like being stone cold sober amidst a group of euphoric drunks who think they're being witty," I said.

"Eat some brownies," he counseled.

When I arrived I sank onto one end of the leather sofa and listened. The group had divided itself as always into small talk-units of two or three, and fragments of the conversation eddied around.

Said a sixty-year-old with bouncy jet-black hair arranged in a Prince Valiant hairdo: "Personally, I think the Accu-jac is the greatest invention since the wheel." And to someone's query about what it was, he explained, "A human ... er ... milking machine. After everything's over, you turn it off. It doesn't go on talking."

From another angle: "—the ego should have a cutoff switch when you're cruising, for only the id is working then ..."

And another: "I liked what he said on the tube about chickenhawks: I can't imagine having an affair with someone to whom you have to explain what you're doing, or gasp physiological instructions such as *higher* or *lower*."

Or: "When he interviewed me he wanted to know why—back in the twenties—I didn't join my 'oppressed brothers and sisters in marching for our rights'! Jaysus! Marching where? For what purpose? To protest to whom? We'd have been jailed. We were too busy having fun, keeping our

134

secret hidden. It was more amusing before the closet opened and so many came out noisy. So much stompin' around."

Beside me, someone said: "When you come, the British call it 'changing the acid.' Kinda cute."

From the depths of an armchair: "My favorite age is the far end of the twenties, just when they're beginning to rot. But I will say the only pleasure in growing old is watching the young and arrogant ones go to pieces."

Faintly, from a corner: " . . . astrology's just medieval clap-trap. In two thousand years they've added two new signs— or should have—the whale and the serpent-slayer. Anyone who believes in astrology is right up there with the medieval scientists who swore that menstrual blood killed grass, tar-nished mirrors, and poisoned iron."

From a straight chair: "I was unpacking my suitcase in Paris and Jacques Guerre was there watching me, and when I came to a box of Band-Aids he kept staring at it and finally he asked what it was, and I told him 'little *pansements* for cuts and scratches' and then it dawned on me: 'bander' in French means *to get a hardon* and 'aid' from 'aider,' *to help*, so Band-Aids in French means something to help you get a hardon."

These statements did not come bang-bang; they were picked from the gossip of a half hour. The first brownie I had eaten began to make itself known. The host's cat sat staring at me. I was not overly fond of cats since I had long ago decided they came from outer space and would eventually take over the world.

J. Brian, one of the porno kings of northern California, approached the sofa with a curly-haired young man in tow. Brian always brought the best.

The young man had broad sweet eyelids, luxurious soft yellow hair with twining rich golden curling spirals, a subtle promising mouth, refined and expressive hands, and supple limbs. Dreamstuff of soft cornflower violet came from his eyes. I looked at him; I heard a lion roar. His body and soul were aflame and aflower in their day of perfection; he was beauty militant and all-conquering. As I watched him, I felt as I used to when I was drinking: I was a prince of the world and commanded fire and flames! It was possible, I decided on the spot, to love physically with a psychic delight—as I loved flowers and white wine and soaring wings and rare perfumes, but anxiously, since human things can hurt. I concluded that in love only the aristocrats understand each other, and there is a laity that knows nothing but physical desire.

"This is Scott," Brian said.

"Hello," I said, and shook hands. Scott pulled a footstool close and sat disturbingly near my knee, which I moved aside a half inch.

"Brian tells me you've written a lot of things as Phil Andros," he said.

"Guilty," I said.

"And that you knew Gertrude and Alice and wrote a book about them, *Dear Sammy*." He inflected the title as if he were addressing me rather than naming the book.

"I haven't read it yet," he went on, "but I'm going to get it, and then will you sign it for me?"

"Sure," I said. My heart was acting strangely.

"I've been collecting autographs," he said. "I've got Tennessee Williams, George Maharis, lots of others. Even Herb Caen. Will you give me yours if I get a piece of paper?"

"Well, I—" I began. "Sure," I said. "Delighted."

He was gone, and came back in a moment with a three by five card. I wrote his name on it, and then in French: "En souvenir d'une nuit de folie à St. Tropez" and signed it.

"Just dandy," he said, with a small wrinkling of his nose. "Now what does it mean?"

"It means 'In memory of a night of madness at St. Tropez,'" I said. "Let's see you explain that to your roommate."

He moved his head slightly, looking down, a charming gesture, and then there came to me one of those magic moments when the cigarette smoke vanished and the sounds of babbling were sucked down into a silence that only I was aware of while a long-forgotten sentence from a book on Leonardo appeared in my mind: *Sometimes a*

gesture or an expression of youth is so charged with physical
grace that it takes the heart with intolerable tenderness, like
the last fine ghost of a wave vanishing on silver sand, or the
young moon shy in a jasper evening . . .

I recalled myself with difficulty, to find him watching me
somewhat enigmatically, the hint of a smile quirking the
corner of his lips. And that turned me to thinking of the
saintly old Arab who was once asked to imagine himself in a
garden of roses and hyacinths with the evening breeze
waving the cypress, and a fair youth of twenty beside him,
with the assurance of perfect privacy . . . "And what then,"
asked the questioner, "would be the result?"

The holy man bowed his head and thought for a moment,
and too honest to lie said finally, "Allah defend me from
such temptation."

"Let me give you my phone number," said Scott, and did,
whereupon I passed him one of my cards.

These small exchanges did not go unnoticed by the crowd,
and I saw one or two looking daggers at me. Prince Valiant
gnawed his lower lip.

"I'd like to come to see you," Scott said.

"By all means." If I had had a green feathered fan, I probably would have batted my eyes at him over the top of it.

The entire episode left me in a tumult. On the way home
Don said, "You really seemed to be making out with the
handsomest one there."

I yawned, pretending boredom. "Somewhat young," I
said.

A few days later Scott came to see me, to get the copy of
Dear Sammy signed. With him he brought a brochure
printed in color, advertising a porno film in which he had
appeared. He gave me also a large color photograph of
himself, naked, with one arm uplifted to a branch, his lithe
tanned swimmer's body amidst a total background of
greenery—cedars and firs—his genitals barely showing
before merging with the green out of which his body sprang.
On the back of it he wrote: "I enjoy your company, and look
forward to more visits in the future. I hope to be as charming
and witty as you are when I am past thirty!"

The net, alas! had fallen on me, for the first time in twenty years. And I was not helped by a drama that appeared on the idiot tube that very night. It was about a female college teacher of ancient history who took in a student roomer. And the handsome student, rummaging in a closet one day, came across a scrapbook which told him that the teacher, the loner, the aloof one, was really in the past the lady member of a song-and-dance vaudeville team. She became emotionally enmeshed with the young man, and he finally moved out—not ever suspecting until the final scene that she had felt something more than affection for him.

It underlined the business of myself and Scott, and was a miniature of the problem that looms large for every aging homosexual. In what year does a good man stop it all? It seemed somehow unfair to me that so late in life I should once more be put through the—well, *agony* was not the word; *annoyance* might be more fitting—of having my emotions churned once again. Could I ever approach the yellow-haired beauty? Where was dignity? Where was pride? I did not want rejection—could not endure it, perhaps. What did I want? the thing that bedevils every homosexual—the one-time physical contact, the dirty five minutes? Did I want friendship? That fades. "Love" was out of the question, and anyway, it dies. What did the student say to the teacher of ancient history? "Affection continues"—but there should be a stronger word than affection—a special word to hold all the yearning for what is lost, all the love for physical beauty, or beauty of mind and intelligence, all the adoration that an older man can have for a younger. There was a new word—"limerence"—lovesickness, which certainly did describe me, for I was lovesmitten. But what was it that I felt for Scott? Or what did he feel for me—if anything?

I found myself wondering about happiness, and the pursuit we make of it—so frantic and unceasing. "If I were as happy now as I was then," we say, sighing. But the truth is that few men have more to their account than a total of a dozen hours of happiness in a lifetime—a fragment here

138

and there out of the dull and sullen roll of years. It is necessary to realize that a state of unhappiness or frustration is the usual lot of nearly all men, nearly all of the time. For most, life is a state of barely endurable discomfort.

Had Scott with his lithe and handsome body, and his color brochure, wrecked everything that I thought had been built so rigid and strong? There in those glowing pages his body was laid out, his dimensions revealed, his activity everything that had come to be expected in a homosexual adult film. The mechanics of all kinds of sex were not foreign to him. But if a shy and tentative first touch from me caused his hand to fall on mine and gently push it aside, could I survive? Could I divorce old barren Reason from my bed?

There is a widespread myth among homosexuals that many find comforting—that there exist great numbers of young men who are fascinated with older ones, aged ones, father-images. I am convinced this is nonsense, a kind of desperate wish-fulfillment, an enamel over the rot of Time. I have seldom seen it—perhaps with Christopher and Don. Yet I remembered that when I was about Scott's age, I sought out three aged men, for varying reasons: Lord Alfred Douglas, a consul-general in Marseille, and an elderly bookseller in Chicago. Aside from the linkage to Oscar Wilde, what was the motivation for the others? Pity? Compassion?

Well, at any rate . . . Nowadays I see Scott frequently. The problem has at last been solved. Once in a while we go to dinner. Occasionally he brings me a small "corsage" of chrysanthemums and tells me—laughing—that I'm his date. He visits me on his bicycle—in a tight red T-shirt and tight short red pants, his long and lovely tanned legs like a flower-stem to a red calyx, his yellow hair and handsome face a part of the flower. His crinkly snippets of hair shine from a reliquary next to Valentino's.

There are times in one's life when you accept the gifts from the gods, and smile, and do not question.

Chapter X

CODA: DETACHMENT

THE BUTTERFLY IS ANCESTRAL TO our personalities. We are always searching for new shepherds in our pastures. Momentarily with one for a few ecstatic moments, we pass to the next with starry eyes raised to the forever unattainable goal, for most of us: our ideal, our "great dark man." But there is always something wrong: he smokes, or he doesn't smoke; he likes this or that food; he taps his fingers or his foot. Our chiefest aim is novelty. We hover at one flower for a moment, extract its sweetness, and go on to the next.

Keats once wrote a letter to his brother in which he praised what he called *negative capability*—a willingness to live in the midst of doubts and uncertainties without any irritable reaching out after fact and reason, never trying to reduce our universe to a neat $x^2 + y^2$ formula. And if we could take that as a starting point, the next step should come easily: the attempt to settle oneself into a pattern which would permit observation—even participation—but still allow detachment, untouched in the deeply emotional sense so that no person or thing or situation would ever have the power again to wound. Such an action might be looked upon as "self-ish," perhaps, making use of the same sort of "self-ness" that underlies our instinct for self-preservation. We look at the label to make sure the bottle does not contain cyanide.

If we cannot detach outselves—what then? The endless empty hours of cruising bars, of suffering from the dwindling number of admirers as we grow older, of the frantic-pathetic efforts to stay young and attractive in a culture which admires youth alone, of not being able to see *le moment juste* when we must renounce the chase, the hopeless pursuit.

To achieve this inner detachment there must be a careful preparation, creation and stocking of inner resources, building them over the years—perhaps a love of music, of books, of art, of anything in which real interest is possible. Pascal once said that the great fault of modern man was that he had to be active, to be *chasing*—after horses, women, excitement of some kind—whereas, he added, if he but realized, he could sit alone in a room and indulge in the wildest and most passionate activity known to man—that of thinking.

For that, however, we need all the inner resources, or at the very least a treasury of memories to sustain us. Since our emotional lives are fragmented, we should have a vast stock of tangible things to invest our love in: mementos, memorabilia, photographs, an old blue cloak (like Newman), a water glass his lips had touched, anything which can stimulate us, can make us remember.

There would be no reason for me to be sardonic about Newman's old blue cloak when remembering my own collection of memorabilia. What of the pale blue-green lachrymatory dating from the third century B.C., found in Athens—turned iridescent by the many tears it had held, for births, unhappy loves, and deaths of athletes? Included among my touchstones are pieces of porphyry from the steam room of the Baths of Caracalla in Rome; all I have to do is to hold one between my fingers to feel the hot juices and waters of the handsome young men slide down between my cracks, or see the crumbling ruins under moonlight with nightingales. There is the stone from Hadrian's villa, the coins from the reigns of Caligula and Elagabalus, the sealed potpourri of rose petals from Gertrude Stein's garden at Bilignin, the gilt sabot that Jean Marais pinned on my lapel, the pubic hair from Valentino along with the dried ferns from his crypt and the leaves from Falcon's Lair, a dictator's breakfast napkin, a seven-inch heavy solid brass anchor given me by a sailor from the *Enterprise*, which he had molded from a used shell casing, a purplish magenta ceramic rose stolen from the ledge of Oscar Wilde's tomb in Père-Lachaise cemetery, a huge plaster reproduction of the Faun of Praxiteles lugged home from Paris in 1939, Alice Toklas' tomato knife, horsehairs from Stein's sofa, Gertrude's stampbox (and scarves from each of them), the small glass intaglios that Sir Francis Rose gave me, the hundred police patches, and twenty hats (those of a Danish cop, a navy captain, a Parisian *pompier*, a San Francisco fuzz, a construction hardhat—and sailors' hats, both white and blue and American and German and French, the cap of a Greek policeman, a *Normandie* steward, a "super" in *The Student Prince*, and both the fatigue and dress hats of our noble marines). Add to these a *canivet*, a pinprick portrait of Voltaire done by the nuns of Cirey in 1750 and given to me by Alice Toklas, and the ancient key to the *latrinenhaus* of the Chateau de Chillon, and you would have enough to live on the rest of your life.

Paradoxically, along with detachment comes a growth of empathy; and with increasing ease you find it possible to make a psychic projection of yourself into the personalities of others. And finally you become aware of the existence of a goal, and reach it easily: when experience has multiplied itself to such an extent that you are no longer under any compulsion of any kind towards persons or things or situations. And then you have the only kind of freedom worth aiming for, and the best reward.

Then you can truly say that you are alive, and that you are living.

INDEX

da Vinci, Leonardo, 75, 106, 136–37
Davis and Elkins College (West Virginia), 31, 37
Dear Sammy (Steward), 68, 136, 137
Dellenback, William, 97, 102
Der Kreis (The Circle), 108–111, 115
Detachment, 140–42
Dickinson, Emily, 21
Dietzel, Amund, 80
Dogs, 130–32
Dougherty, Cyril, 7
Douglas, Lord Alfred, 44–51, 57, 139
Doyle, Peter, 18, 106
Dreiser, Theodore, 21, 56
Drinking, 6–7, 34, 51, 58, 65, 102

Ellis, Havelock, 12, 14, 18, 95
eos, 111
Everybody's Autobiography (Stein), 65

Faulkner, William, 56
Finnegans Wake (Joyce), 76
Fraternities, 23–24
Freud, Sigmund, 21, 44, 74, 95

Garbo, Greta, 21, 26
Garland, Hamlin, 45, 46
Gebhard, Paul, 100
Genet, Jean, 97, 101, 114
Gide, André, 44, 46, 47, 49, 50, 52–58
Gillespie, Jon, 27
Glacier Park (Montana), 35–37
Goddard, Lucy, 4
Gold, Michael, 56, 71
Grapes of Wrath, The (Steinbeck), 56
Graves, William L. ("Billy"), 19

Greek Way, The (Andros/Steward), 117
Griffin, Russell, 27
Griffith, Ella, 4
Gwendolyn, 8

Harris, Frank, 47, 49
Hatcher, Harlan H., 28–29
Hells Angels, 90–92
Hemingway, Ernest, 21, 48, 56
Hero, destruction of the, 82–83
Holland, E. O., 37–39
Homosexuality, 1–142
Housman, A. E., 37, 44, 46
Huysmans, Joris-Karl, 27–28, 29–30

Ida, 34
Ides of March, The (Wilder), 76–77
Immoralist, The (Gide), 52, 56
Innocents of Paris, The (Andrews), 20
Institute for Sex Research, 97, 100–101
Invert, The ("Anomaly"), 19

Jerusalem (Ohio), 5
Johnson, Clifford L., 10–11, 15
Joy Spot, The (Andros/Steward), 116
Jung, Rudolf, 110

Kahane, Jack, 97
Kathryn, 9, 13
Kent, Kim, 111–12, 113–14
Kinsey, Alfred C., 80, 81, 95–106, 108
Kipling, Rudyard, 48
Ku Klux Klan, 5

Leaves of Grass (Whitman), 18–19
Lesbians, 63

Other Grey Fox Books

Daniel Curzon   *Human Warmth & Other Stories*

Allen Ginsberg   *Composed on the Tongue*
                     Gates of Wrath
                     Gay Sunshine Interview
                     (with Allen Young)

Howard Griffin   *Conversations with W. H. Auden*

Richard Hall   *Couplings, A Book of Stories*

Frank O'Hara   *Early Writing*
                     Poems Retrieved
                     Standing Still and Walking
                     in New York

Michael Rumaker   *A Day and a Night at the Baths*
                     My First Satyrnalia

Allen Young   *Gays Under the Cuban Revolution*